Tempted by Midnight

A Midnight Breed Novella

By Lara Adrian

1001 Dark Nights

EVIL EYE
CONCEPTS

Tempted by Midnight
A Midnight Breed Novella
By Lara Adrian

1001 Dark Nights
Copyright 2014 Lara Adrian LLC
ISBN: 978-1-940887-09-8

Foreword: Copyright 2014 M. J. Rose
Published by Evil Eye Concepts, Incorporated

Sign up for the 1001 Dark Nights Newsletter and be entered to win a Tiffany Key necklace.

There's a contest every month!

Go to www.1001DarkNights.com to subscribe.

As a bonus, all subscribers will receive a free 1001 Dark Nights story on 1/1/15.
The First Night
by Shayla Black, Lexi Blake & M.J. Rose

One Thousand and One Dark Nights

Once upon a time, in the future...

*I was a student fascinated with stories and learning.
I studied philosophy, poetry, history, the occult, and
the art and science of love and magic. I had a vast
library at my father's home and collected thousands
of volumes of fantastic tales.*

*I learned all about ancient races and bygone
times. About myths and legends and dreams of all
people through the millennium. And the more I read
the stronger my imagination grew until I discovered
that I was able to travel into the stories... to actually
become part of them.*

*I wish I could say that I listened to my teacher
and respected my gift, as I ought to have. If I had, I
would not be telling you this tale now.
But I was foolhardy and confused, showing off
with bravery.*

*One afternoon, curious about the myth of the
Arabian Nights, I traveled back to ancient Persia to
see for myself if it was true that every day Shahryar
(Persian: شهريار, "king") married a new virgin, and then
sent yesterday's wife to be beheaded. It was written
and I had read, that by the time he met Scheherazade,*

the vizier's daughter, he'd killed one thousand women.

Something went wrong with my efforts. I arrived in the midst of the story and somehow exchanged places with Scheherazade — a phenomena that had never occurred before and that still to this day, I cannot explain.

Now I am trapped in that ancient past. I have taken on Scheherazade's life and the only way I can protect myself and stay alive is to do what she did to protect herself and stay alive.

Every night the King calls for me and listens as I spin tales. And when the evening ends and dawn breaks, I stop at a point that leaves him breathless and yearning for more. And so the King spares my life for one more day, so that he might hear the rest of my dark tale.

As soon as I finish a story... I begin a new one... like the one that you, dear reader, have before you now.

CHAPTER 1

He had lived for more than a thousand years, long enough that few things still held the power to amaze him. The sea at night was one of those rare pleasures for Lazaro Archer.

Standing on the third-level bow deck of a gleaming, 279-foot private megayacht off the western coast of Italy, Lazaro braced his hands on the polished mahogany rail and indulged his senses in a brief appreciation of his moonlit surroundings.

Crisp, salty Mediterranean air filled his nostrils and tousled his jet-black hair. The late summer breeze was cool tonight, gusting rhythmically toward the Italian mainland. Dark, rippling water spread out in all directions under the milky glow of the cloud-strewn moon and blanket of stars. Far below, waves lapped fluidly, sensually, against the sides of the yacht where it floated, engines silenced as it waited at its destined location on the Tyrrhenian Sea.

Lazaro supposed the luxurious vessel he stood aboard would take the breath away from just about anyone—human or Breed. Being born the latter, and first generation Breed besides, one of the vampire nation's eldest, most pure-blooded individuals, Lazaro had known his fair share of wealth and luxury.

He'd once had all of those things himself. Still did, if he could be bothered to care.

He left everything he once had back in Boston twenty years ago, after the most precious things in his long life had been taken from him. His blood-bonded Breedmate, his sons and their mates, a houseful of innocent children...all gone. His only surviving kin was his grandson, Kellan, who'd been with Lazaro the night the Archers' Darkhaven home was razed to the ground in a heinous, unprovoked attack by a madman named Dragos.

Lazaro exhaled deeply, no longer feeling the raw scrape of grief whenever he thought of his slain family. The anguish had dulled over time, yet his guilt was always with him, scarred over like a physical wound. A hideous, permanent reminder of his loss.

Of his life's greatest failure.

If his existence had any meaning now, it belonged to his work with Lucan Thorne and his fellow Breed warriors of the Order. As the commander of the Order's operation in Rome these past two decades, Lazaro had little time for self-pity or personal indulgences. He had even less opportunity for pleasure, rare or otherwise.

Which was the way he preferred it.

He dealt in justice now.

At times, he dealt in death.

Tonight, he was representing the Order on a less official basis, on the hopes that he could facilitate a secret meeting between two of his trusted friends. One of them was Breed, a high-ranking American member of the Global Nations Council. The other, the megayacht's owner, was human, an influential

Italian businessman who also happened to be the brother of that country's newly elected president, a politician who had won his office with tough talk against the Breed. If the meeting with Paolo Turati took place as planned tonight and was deemed a success, it would be the first step toward forging an alliance with one of the vampire nation's most vocal detractors.

As for Byron Walsh, the Breed male had been one of Lazaro's colleagues in the States, even before the GNC had tapped Walsh for his current diplomatic post. As leader of his own Darkhaven in Maryland, Walsh's social circle had occasionally intersected with Lazaro's in Boston. There had even been a time, one bitter winter, that Walsh's family came to visit Lazaro's at their Back Bay mansion.

A long time ago, back when Lazaro had a Darkhaven. Back when he still had a family kept safe under his protection.

It had been even longer since Lazaro Archer had played emissary for any cause. He hoped like hell this clandestine introduction wasn't a mistake.

Seventy-odd miles behind him was the seaside town of Anzio, where Lazaro had joined Turati on his yacht a couple of hours ago. Up ahead of them, an even farther distance, the island of Sardinia glittered with light against the darkness.

A smattering of other large yachts and watercraft bobbed in the vast space between Turati's vessel and the island, but it was the low drone of a motorboat that captured Lazaro's full attention. The size of a small cabin cruiser, the yacht tender had departed from an idling vessel in the distance and was heading Lazaro's way. He watched the chase boat approach from out of the inky darkness, its navigation lights dimmed as instructed, flashing three times as it crossed the water toward them.

His Breed colleague from the States did not disappoint. Byron Walsh was arriving as promised, and right on time.

Lazaro nodded, grim with relief.

He turned away from the rail and headed down to the yacht's main deck salon where Turati waited. On Lazaro's directions and assurances, the gray-haired billionaire had brought just two men from his usual security entourage. The yacht's crew of fifty had been reduced to a bare dozen, just enough personnel to operate the vessel.

At Lazaro's entrance to the lavish salon, Turati glanced up, wiry brows lifting in question. "He comes?" the old man asked in his native tongue.

Lazaro answered in Italian as well. "The boat is on the way now." As tonight's host did not speak English, Lazaro would personally translate for the duration of the meeting, if only to ensure that the conversation didn't inadvertently stray into unfriendly waters.

Paolo Turati was one of a small number of humans Lazaro considered a friend. He was also one of the few humans who didn't look upon the Breed as a race of monsters in need of collaring at best, or, at worst, wholesale extermination.

Granted, the fear wasn't without cause. For millennia, the Breed existed in the shadows alongside their *Homo sapiens* neighbors. In the twenty years since Lazaro's kind was outed to man, trust between the two races on the planet had been anything but easy.

That trust became even more complicated a couple of weeks ago, when a violent cabal calling themselves Opus Nostrum smuggled a bomb into a very important summit gathering of Breed and human dignitaries.

If tonight's introductions went well, the Breed would gain a supportive voice and a much-needed ally in their efforts to keep the peace between man and vampire all around the world. If it went poorly, the Order's efforts to broker peace could ignite the smoldering war that Opus Nostrum seemed to want so badly.

"I hope your friend from Maryland comes to this meeting with the same intentions as I do," Turati said, apprehension in the flat line of his mouth, even though the old human's eyes held Lazaro in a trusting look. "If I like what I hear tonight, I will do what I can to persuade my brother to at least entertain the idea of talks with the GNC and Lucan Thorne. After all, everyone's goal is peace, not only for ourselves, but for our generations to follow."

"Indeed," Lazaro replied. His acute Breed hearing picked up the faint, approaching growl of the boat carrying Byron Walsh. "He's arriving now. Wait here, Paolo. I'll go down to meet him and bring him up."

Turati frowned then shook his head. "I will join you, Lazaro. It seems only proper that I greet Councilman Walsh personally and welcome him aboard along with you. I would do no less for any invited guest."

Lazaro inclined his head in agreement. "A fine idea."

He waited patiently as the old man stood and smoothed his custom-tailored navy suit and creamy silk shirt. By contrast, Lazaro was dressed in what he'd come to regard as *Order casual*—black slacks, light-duty combat boots, and a fitted black patrol shirt.

And although he was first generation Breed and more than deadly with his bare hands alone, he carried a blade concealed in each boot and had a semiautomatic 9mm pistol strapped to his right ankle. He didn't expect trouble from either of the two men or their few staff present at tonight's meeting, but he'd be damned if he didn't come prepared for it.

Together, he and Turati left the grand salon on the yacht's second level, making their way down a polished brass stairwell that spiraled elegantly onto the lower deck. The boat carrying

Walsh was coming around the stern as Lazaro and Turati arrived on the aft deck to meet it.

A suited bodyguard stood at attention on the motorboat, just outside the cabin's hatch. He was Breed, as big and menacing as any one of Lazaro's kind. Turati's steps hesitated at the sight of the unsmiling guard. The two men comprising the Italian's own security detail now stood behind their employer, pulses spiking with a tension Lazaro felt as a palpable vibration in the air.

He gave a solemn nod of greeting to Walsh's guard, the signal as good as his word that Walsh would be safe among friends tonight. The guard turned, opened the hatch to murmur an "all clear" to the boat's occupants.

Byron Walsh appeared in that next instant. Dressed less formally than Turati, the Breed diplomat emerged from the cabin in a crisp white shirt with rolled-back sleeves and fawn-colored slacks. Although Walsh was formidable-looking, over six feet tall and heavily muscled, like all of their kind, his relaxed attire softened his edges.

As did the smile he gave as he disembarked from his tender and stepped onto the deck of Turati's yacht. Walsh's friendliness seemed genuine, even if his smile didn't quite reach his eyes. There was an undercurrent of anxiety about him, as if he hadn't yet decided if he was stepping onto safe ground or a nest of vipers.

"Lazaro, my old friend, it's been too long. Good to see you," he greeted briefly, then extended his hand to the evening's host. *"Signor Turati, buona sera."*

"Paolo," Turati offered as the two men shook hands.

"Thank you for agreeing to this meeting," Walsh continued in English. "And please forgive the cloak-and-dagger aspect of our introduction tonight. Unfortunately, there are those who might prefer to keep our people at odds, rather than embrace the peace that you and I both hope to achieve."

Lazaro murmured a quick translation, to which Turati smiled and replied in kind. "Paolo says he is honored to have the opportunity to talk and share ideas with you, Byron. He would like you and your men to be comfortable as his guests inside now."

Walsh held up his hand, gesturing to wait. "A moment, if you will. We're not all present just yet." He pivoted to look at his pair of Breed bodyguards behind him. "Where's Mel?"

"Right behind me a second ago," one of his men answered.

Lazaro scowled, confused, and not a little concerned that Walsh had apparently brought a third member of his entourage when the agreement had explicitly called for balance on both sides of this informal summit. He shot a questioning glower at his friend—just as a head emerged from the cabin below.

A head covered in long, luscious waves of fiery red hair.

"I'm sorry," the woman offered hastily as she made her way out. "I had to sit down for a second. I'm afraid I'm still trying to find my sea legs."

She came out of the cabin completely then, and every pair of eyes on deck rooted onto her like the tide pulled toward the moon. Not even Lazaro was immune.

Christ, not even close.

"Ah. There you are, darling." Walsh pivoted to assist her off the smaller vessel.

Darling? Lazaro vaguely recalled hearing that Byron Walsh had lost his mate in a car accident three or four years ago. Had he taken another lover so soon? Whether she was a Breedmate or human female, Lazaro couldn't be sure.

More to the point, what the hell was Walsh thinking, showing up with her unexpectedly to a meeting of this importance? Lazaro had worked on Paolo Turati for months before the man finally agreed to open the door to talks with a member of the GNC. Walsh himself had been reluctant to trust the kin of a government leader who made no secret of his suspicion and distaste for the entire population of the Breed. Lazaro could not imagine what had possessed Walsh to treat this unofficial summit as a goddamned pleasure cruise.

If grabbing the Breed male by the throat and demanding an answer to that very question wouldn't turn an already awkward situation into a potential disaster, Lazaro might have uncurled his fists at his sides and done just that. Instead, he stared, silent and fuming. He'd deal with his friend's apparent lapse in judgment later.

"Careful now," Walsh cautioned his uninvited companion. "Watch your step, sweetheart."

Hell, every male present was watching her step. She was tall, elegant, with bountiful curves that filled out every body-skimming line of a conservative—yet damned sexy—charcoal gray skirt that skimmed her knees and showcased her long, shapely legs. She wore a garnet-colored silk blouse unbuttoned midway down her sternum, just low enough to tease at the generous swell of her bosom.

At the base of her throat was a small scarlet birthmark in the shape of a teardrop falling into the cradle of a crescent moon. So, the voluptuous beauty was a Breedmate, Lazaro noted with displeasure. Had she been simply human arm candy for the councilman, Lazaro would have no qualms at all about turning her sinfully formed behind right back around and sending the motorboat away with her inside.

But a female born with the Breedmate mark commanded deeper respect than that from one of Lazaro's kind. And although he was more warrior now than gentleman, there was still a part of him that held rare females like this one in high regard. And if she was in fact mated to Byron Walsh, then Lazaro had no bloody right to stare at her with a smoldering crackle of interest heating his veins.

As her slender-heeled pumps settled gracefully on the deck, she lifted her head and glanced up to look at him and the other men. Her mane of lustrous, flame-bright hair framed a delicate oval face dominated by large green eyes and soft, sensual lips.

She was, in a word, stunning.

The face of an angel and the kind of body to tempt a saint.

And based on the sudden hush of focused male interest on the deck of Turati's yacht, there was hardly a saint among them.

Lazaro shut down his own awareness of her with abrupt, violent force.

Walsh took the woman's hand and led her forward. "Lazaro, you'll remember my daughter, Mel."

In a flash of memory, Lazaro envisioned a gangly tomboy about seven years old who'd come with her adopted parents to the Archer Darkhaven one winter. Freckle-faced, scrawny, and possessed of more courage than good sense, the way he recalled it now.

Nothing like the curvaceous, poised woman he saw before him here.

"Melena," she corrected her father gently, her lush mouth bowing in a polite smile as she offered her hand in greeting first to Turati, then to Lazaro. "I'm my father's personal assistant. Tonight I'll also be translating for him." She turned the full strength of her smile on Turati, speaking now in flawless Italian. "I hope you don't mind. Between you and me, Daddy's Italian is only slightly better than his French, which isn't saying much."

Turati chuckled, his aged eyes twinkling as he drank in the sight of Melena Walsh. The pair immediately began a light, effusive chat about Italy and its numerous areas of superiority over all things French. Lazaro didn't want to be impressed with the young woman, but he couldn't deny her language skills—or her charm. Paolo Turati was no pushover and it had taken her less than a minute to have the old goat eating out of the palm of her soft white hand.

Still, this wasn't a social call.

There was real business to be done tonight.

Lazaro cleared his throat in effort to break up the uninvited distraction. "Your offer to translate is appreciated, Miss Walsh—"

"Melena, please," she interjected.

"But it won't be necessary," Lazaro finished. "As this meeting is confidential and a matter of global security as well, all interpretation will be handled personally by me. I trust you understand."

She glanced at her father, an anxious flick of her eyes.

"I'll be more comfortable knowing Mel is nearby," Walsh replied. "As you say, Lazaro, there is much at stake in the world, and I would hate for my clumsy words to convey anything less than what I truly mean. Likewise, before I leave tonight, I would like to be sure that I've understood everything Paolo intends me to know."

"You don't trust that I am capable of assuring you of both those things?"

"Melena's come all this way to assist me, Lazaro."

"And she's welcome to wait on board in one of the other salons until the meeting is finished." Lazaro met his old friend's gaze, tried to decipher some of the apprehension he saw in the Breed male's eyes. "If you don't like my decision, take it up with Lucan Thorne when you return to the States."

Turati was frowning now, lost by the rapid back-and-forth

in English. "Something is wrong?" he asked, directing his question to Lazaro in Italian, even though he could hardly tear his gaze away from Melena. "Tell me what is going on."

"Miss Walsh will join us after the meeting concludes," Lazaro informed him. "She was unaware of the sensitive nature of this arrangement and has agreed that I should provide the necessary translation assistance as planned."

Melena glanced down, and Turati's face pinched into a deeper frown. He stepped toward her, his mouth pursing under his silent contemplation. When she looked up at him, the old man grinned, hooking a thumb in Lazaro's direction. "Shall we ask him to join us after the meeting instead?" he whispered in Italian. "I would much rather listen to your voice for the next few hours than his, my dear."

She smiled but started to shake her head. "Thank you, Mr. Turati, but I cannot—"

"You can, and I insist that you do. You and your father are both my guests here tonight. I'll banish neither of you from our meeting." Turati slanted a sly glance at Lazaro. "I won't banish you either. Come, let's go inside now."

Lazaro sent the motor boat away with a dismissing wave as he waited for the Walshes, Turati, and the two pairs of bodyguards to head back up to the yacht's main salon. Then, with a low curse and a vague, but troubled, niggling in his veins, he fell in behind them.

CHAPTER 2

The meeting was going far better than they could have hoped. Especially considering Melena had nearly been banned from the room before it even started.

Her father and Paolo Turati had talked without interruption for a couple of hours—serious conversations ranging from cultural misconceptions among the Breed and mankind, to the volatile political climate that existed between the two races. They'd discussed their hopes for a better future and confessed their shared worries about what that future might look like if the mistrust that festered on either side of Breed/human relations were allowed to continue.

Or worse, if it were encouraged to spread—something the failed terror act at the GNC peace summit in Washington, D.C., two weeks ago had seemed orchestrated to do.

The two men hadn't solved the world's many problems in the space of two hours, but they did seem to be forming a genuine respect and fondness for each other. With the heavier subjects behind them, Melena happily translated as they moved on to trading anecdotes from recent travels they'd both enjoyed and talk of their children. Mundane, comfortable conversations peppered with easy smiles, even bouts of laughter.

If her father had reservations about his trip overseas for this covert audience, those concerns seemed all but evaporated now. And he had been more than apprehensive, Melena had to admit. He'd been on the verge of paranoia in the days leading up to this meeting.

He worried that betrayal awaited him around every corner— not so much groundless panic, but a hunch he couldn't shake. Born with limited precognitive ability, her father's hunches, good or bad, all too often proved to be fact.

Every Breed vampire was gifted with a preternatural talent unique to himself. The same held true for Breedmates like Melena, women who bore the teardrop-and-crescent-moon mark and had the rare genetic makeup that allowed them to blood-bond with one of the Breed in an eternal union and bear his young.

It was Melena's specific extrasensory ability that brought her along with her father tonight, more so than her translation skills. She'd needed to see Paolo Turati in person in order to assure her father of the human's intentions. And she'd been satisfied in that regard. *Signor* Turati was a good man, one who could be trusted at his word.

Melena was glad she could be there to allay her father's worry, even if her presence had met with the glowering disapproval of the Breed male who'd arranged the important introduction.

For the duration of the meeting so far, Lazaro Archer had loomed in brooding silence at the peripheral of the megayacht's opulent main deck salon, as distracting as a dark storm cloud. While he'd allowed her to translate as Turati insisted, it was obvious the raven-haired Gen One Breed male wasn't happy about it.

No, he was furious. He wanted her gone. And she didn't need to rely on ESP to tell her so.

From the sharp stab of his piercing indigo gaze, which had been fixed on her each time she dared a look in his direction, Melena guessed it wasn't often he found himself not in absolute control of any given situation.

She could personally attest to Lazaro Archer's commanding, take-charge demeanor. She had witnessed him in action firsthand once. She'd been just a child, but to say he left an impression was an understatement.

Memory yanked her back to a cold winter night and a foolish dare gone terribly wrong. She could still feel the frozen water engulf her. Could still see the blackness that filled her vision as her head struck something hard and sharp with her fall.

Idly, Melena ran her fingertips across the scar that cut a fine line through her left eyebrow. She didn't realize she was being spoken to until she saw both her father and Paolo Turati looking at her in expectation.

"Oh, I...I'm sorry," she stammered, embarrassed to have been caught drifting. Especially with Lazaro Archer there to notice it too. "Would you repeat that last part for me, please? I want to be certain I get it correct."

Her father chuckled. "Sweetheart, I just asked if you might like to take a short break. We've been going on for hours without a rest. I'm sure we all could use a few minutes to relax a bit."

"Of course," she replied, then pivoted to translate for their smiling host.

As she rose from the antique sofa, both men politely stood with her. Lazaro Archer took the opportunity to stalk out of the salon. She watched him disappear into the darkness outside.

"Would you like some wine?" Turati asked her, his Italian words infused with pride as he gestured to a collection of bottles encased in a lighted cabinet the length of one entire wall of the salon. "My family owns three vineyards, one dating back nearly a thousand years. I would be pleased if you would join me for a glass of my favorite vintage."

Melena smiled back at him. "I would enjoy that very much, thank you. But first, may I ask where I might find a restroom, please?"

"Certainly, certainly." Turati snapped his fingers at the pair of bodyguards who'd been hanging back obediently for the duration of the night. Continuing with Melena in Italian, he said, "There is one just through that door and down the passageway, my dear. Gianni will show you—"

"No, that's okay." She shook her head at the approaching guard, unaccustomed to so much fawning and more than capable of finding her own way. "Thank you, but I'm sure I can find it on my own. Will you all excuse me?"

With a reassuring glance at her father and a nod to Turati, Melena headed out of the salon and into the passageway. The private restroom at the other end was every bit as sumptuous as the salon, with gilded trim and elegant millwork, gleaming mirrors, and a wealth of original art on the walls.

As she came out of the single stall a few moments later and washed her hands, she couldn't help but pause to check her reflection in the polished glass. Her light copper hair was wind-tossed and thickened from the humidity of the sea. Her skin was milky beneath the freckles that spread out over the apples of her cheeks and marched across the bridge of her nose. And the aura that radiated off her was imbued with shades of green and gold.

Hope.

Determination.

She tried not to notice the faint pink glow that simmered beneath the stronger colors of her psyche. Her curiosity about Lazaro Archer had no place here. Her awareness of him as a dark, dangerously attractive male, even less. She'd come to assist her father; that was all.

And besides, the grim representative from the Order had given her no reason to think he'd even noticed her tonight, other than as a nuisance he was eager to relieve himself of at the earliest opportunity.

Every time she looked at him, he'd been cloaked in a haze of unreadable, gunmetal gray. Coupled with his intimidating gaze, the effect should have been enough to make her keep a healthy distance.

Instead, as she left the restroom, rather than returning straight to the salon again, Melena pivoted in the opposite direction. Toward the aft deck, where she'd seen him go.

He stood alone at the rail in the dark, a stoic figure, unmoving, forbidding. His large hands were braced wide before him. His immense, black-clad body leaned slightly forward as he gazed off the stern of the yacht over the endless blanket of rippling water beyond.

Melena took a silent step toward him, then hesitated.

This was probably a bad idea. She should go back inside and focus on what she was supposed to be doing. She had no business with Lazaro Archer, even if there was something she'd been wanting to say to him all night. For much longer than that, in fact.

But from the rigidity of his stance, she could see that he was in no mood for conversation. Probably least of all with the interloper who'd shown up uninvited and inadvertently defied his authority over the meeting.

Her feet paused beneath her, Melena started to pivot around to leave him to his solitude.

"You're doing well in there." His deep voice arrested her where she stood. He didn't bother to look at her, and although the compliment was completely unexpected, it came out more like a growled accusation.

"Thanks." Tentatively, since there was no point in trying to avoid him now, she crossed the deck to join him at the railing. "I like *Signor* Turati. And I have a good feeling about this meeting. I think my father has made a true friend here tonight."

Lazaro grunted. "I'll be sure to inform Lucan Thorne that you give your blessing."

Melena exhaled a short sigh. "I'm not trying to minimize the importance of this meeting. I understand what's at stake—"

"No. You couldn't possibly," he replied, finally swiveling his head to look askance at her.

And oh, Lord. If she thought Lazaro Archer was intimidating from across the room, up close he was terrifying. His midnight-blue eyes glittered as dark as obsidian in the moonlight, ruthless under the ebony slashes of his brows. His strong nose and sharp cheekbones gave him a ferocity no human face could carry off, and his squared, rigid jawline seemed hewn of granite.

Only his mouth had an element of softness to it, though right now, as he looked at her, his broad, sensual lips were flattened in an irritated scowl.

"How old are you?" he demanded.

"Twenty-nine."

He scoffed, his dark gaze giving her a brief once-over. Based on the fierce ticking of a tendon in his already ironclad jaw, she guessed he didn't particularly like what he saw. "You've barely been out of diapers long enough to understand how important it is to have peace between the Breed and humankind. You were only a child when the veil between our world and theirs was torn away. You didn't wade through the blood in the streets. You didn't see the death, the brutality inflicted on so many innocents by both sides of this war." He blew out a curse and shook his head slowly back and forth. "You can't possibly comprehend how thin the thread is that holds back an even uglier war now. Nor can you know the lengths to which some people will go to rip that thread to tatters."

"You're talking about Opus Nostrum," Melena said quietly. A flicker of surprise in those narrowing indigo eyes now. "As my father's personal assistant, he trusts me completely with all of his GNC business. I collect data for him. I summarize reports. I attend most of his meetings, as well as compose the majority of his speeches. I'm also his daughter, so of course, I'm well aware of the attempted bombing at the summit he attended a couple of weeks ago. I know Opus wanted to take a lot of lives at that event—Breed and human. I also know the Order's primary objective now is to unmask the members of Opus's secret cabal and take the terror group down."

Lazaro grunted but seemed less than impressed. "If you came out here to recite your credentials, Miss Walsh, let me spare you the effort."

"You all but challenged me to tell you," she pointed out.

"And all you've done is confirm what I already knew about you. I have a job to do here too, and you've been standing in my way all night." He glanced back out at the water. "I'm sure your ample charms will find a far more receptive audience back in the salon."

Ample charms? Was that a cut on the fact that she actually had curves and a figure, or could he possibly mean he found her even a little bit interesting?

"I didn't come out here to...Jesus, never mind," she stammered. "Forgive me for disturbing you." Frustrated, Melena pushed back from the railing. She started to pivot away, then paused. Glanced over at him one last time, her own anger spiking. "We've met, you know. You don't remember me."

Why she felt stung by that she really didn't want to consider. When he didn't respond after a long moment, she decided it was probably for the best. God knew, she would be better off forgetting the night she nearly died too.

She turned and headed back across the deck.

"I remember a reckless child doing something stupid," he muttered from behind her. "A silly little girl, being somewhere she damned well didn't belong."

Rather like the way he seemed to regard her now, she thought, bristling at the comment.

"I was seven," Melena replied, swinging a look over her shoulder at him. Lazaro hadn't moved from his position, was still staring out at the black water. "I was seven years old, and you saved my life. I'd be dead if not for you."

"Saved you? Christ." He exhaled sharply, as if the idea annoyed him. "I'm not in the habit of saving anyone."

Something about the way he said that, the quieting of his tone, and the almost raw edge to his words made her drift back toward him. She rubbed a chill from her arms as the recollection of her accident washed over her with fresh terror.

"Well, you did save me. You pulled me out of that frozen pond and you saved my life." He didn't look her way at all, hardly acknowledged she had returned. "My family was in Boston, visiting at your Darkhaven. A bunch of us kids were playing outside that night, mostly boys—your grandsons and young nephews and my older brother, Derek. Unlike me, they were all Breed, and as the only girl with them besides, it took all

I had to keep up."

Sometimes she felt as though she were still competing, still struggling to prove her worth in everything she did. She realized she held others up to her same impossible standards too. Her parents had pointed it out to her on numerous occasions. So had more than a few of her exes.

Now here she was, making a point to remind this arrogant man of the stupidest thing she'd ever done in her life.

Melena let out a soft sigh as she stood next to Lazaro once more. "The boys didn't want me there with them at the pond, but I followed them anyway. They started daring each other to walk farther and farther out onto the ice."

"Idiots, all of them," Lazaro grumbled. "Winter came late that year. The pond hadn't yet frozen toward the center."

"Yes," she agreed. "And it was very dark that night. I didn't realize the ice wouldn't hold me until I was already too far out. I stepped onto a thin section, and it broke away underneath me."

The curse Lazaro uttered was ripe, violent. But the look he finally swung on her was oddly tender, haunted. To her complete shock, he reached out and grazed the pad of his thumb over her scarred eyebrow. "You'd hit your head on something."

"The edge of the ice was jagged," she murmured, her throat going a bit dry for the mere second his touch had lingered on her face. When his hand was gone, she shivered, though not from anything close to a chill. "I went down very quickly. God, the water was so cold. I could hardly move my limbs. I panicked. I couldn't see anything. When I tried to swim back up, I realized I was trapped under the ice."

Lazaro was listening intently now, his expression impossible to read. His aura forbid her too, the dull gray haze blurring the edges of his broad shoulders and strong arms, haloing his dangerously handsome face like a brooding cloud against the darkness of the night that surrounded him.

"I remember everything started to go black," Melena said. "And then...there you were. In the water with me, pulling me to the surface. You dived into that frigid pond and searched until you found me. Then you brought me back to your Darkhaven."

"You were bleeding," he said, his gaze returning to the scar above her left eye.

Melena nodded. "Your Breedmate, Ellie, helped my mother patch me up."

Both women were gone now. Melena's adoptive mother, Byron Walsh's mate, Frances, had been killed in a senseless car accident a few years ago. Lazaro's kind-hearted, beautiful Breedmate, Eleanor, had suffered a far more brutal end. Killed just a couple of years after Melena had met her, along with the rest of Lazaro's family who'd been home at his Boston Darkhaven the night of an horrific attack.

His gaze hardened, going distant at the mention of his lost mate. It took nearly all of Melena's self-control to keep from reaching out to offer comfort to him now.

If she didn't think he'd snap her fingers off at the roots, she might have braved it in spite of his forbidding glower.

And yet, there was something more in his eyes as he looked at her. As much as she was drawn to him tonight, she couldn't help feeling that he was aware of her too. Not as the hapless girl he'd fished out of a frozen pond, not even as the grown-up daughter of a colleague and friend.

He was annoyed with her tonight, no question. Given a choice, he'd probably still prefer her gone. But Lazaro Archer was also looking at her the way a man looked at a woman. And she couldn't deny that his interest made her pulse trip into a faster tempo.

"What are you doing here, Melena?" His gruff question caught her off guard.

Did she even know the answer to that? She shrugged lamely. "I guess I just...I don't think I ever got the chance to thank you—"

"No." He cocked his head slightly, those unsettling eyes narrowing shrewdly now. "I mean, what are you doing here at this meeting? As skilled of an interpreter as you are, I think we both know there's something you're not saying."

She stared at him, wondering how he'd gone from looking at her like he wanted to touch her—maybe even kiss her—to pinning her in a suspicious glare. Maybe he hadn't been ignoring her all evening, but silently assessing her, even now.

Part of her wanted to tell him the truth. That she'd been a psychic insurance policy, to make certain her father wasn't walking into a trap with Turati or his men, regardless of the Order's assurances. Lazaro would be furious to hear it, no doubt. That she and her father had defied diplomatic protocol to insert her into a top secret meeting without the knowledge or permission of the Order or the GNC? She didn't even want to consider the ramifications of that, for her or her father.

And anyway, it wasn't her place to publicly voice her father's fears or suspicions, not even to Lazaro Archer. If any of Byron Walsh's colleagues knew how paralyzing his paranoia had become lately, he would surely lose his position on the Council. Her father lived for his work, and Melena would not be the one to jeopardize that for him.

"I don't know what you mean," she murmured, hating that she had to deceive Lazaro. "And I really ought to get back inside now."

"You're protecting him. From what?" Lazaro took hold of her by the arms, preventing her from escaping his knowing stare or his questions. His large hands gripped her firmly, strong fingers searing her with the heat of his touch. "What is your father trying to hide?"

"Nothing, I swear—"

He wasn't buying it. Anger flashed in his eyes. Behind his full upper lip, she glimpsed the sharp points of his emerging fangs. "Tell me what he's afraid of, Melena. Tell me now, before I go in there and haul his ass out here to tell me himself."

"It's nothing," she insisted, finding it impossible to break Lazaro's hold or his stare. "It doesn't matter anyway. He had no reason to be afraid tonight. Turati's intentions are good, he means no harm to—"

She wasn't able to finish what she was saying because in that same instant, Lazaro tensed. His head snapped up, eyes searching the dark sky. Some of the blood seemed to drain out of his grim face in that fraction of a second.

"Fuck," he snarled, his grip tightening on Melena's arms. *"Goddamnit, no."*

He lunged into motion, yanking her against him protectively. His arms wrapped around her. He then tumbled her over the railing of the second-level deck along with him...

Just as a screaming object arrowed down from the sky.

It hit the yacht, a direct, dead center strike.

The vessel exploded. On the deafening boom of impact, Melena crashed into the hard waves with Lazaro. Engulfed by the cold, horrified by what she was seeing, all the air left her lungs on an anguished cry. She tried to break away, but Lazaro held her close, refusing to let her swim back up to find her father.

Together she and Lazaro sank deep into the water, falling down, and down, and down...

Far above them, a hellish ball of flame had erupted on the surface. Fiery chunks of debris dropped into the sea everywhere she looked.

There was only ruin left up there.

The yacht and all of its occupants obliterated in an instant.

CHAPTER 3

By Lazaro's guess, they had been in the water roughly two hours before Anzio's cliff-edged shore was finally within sight. Bleeding from shrapnel wounds and battered by the long journey, he was close to exhaustion—even with the preternatural strength and speed of Breed genetics at his command.

Melena was faring far worse. She was limp against him, having fallen unconscious somewhere around the halfway point of their swim. Although she wasn't entirely mortal either, her human metabolism could not cope with the prolonged exposure in the cold seawater.

In that regard, Lazaro was doubly fortunate. Being Breed had given him another advantage. The same one that had allowed him to pull Melena out of the frozen pond twenty-two years ago. His ability to withstand extreme temperatures had given him the strength to search for her under the ice and pull her to safety before she drowned.

He hoped he hadn't lost her tonight.

Lazaro held her close at his side as he paddled the last few hundred yards with his free arm. As soon as his bare feet were able to touch ground, he repositioned Melena in both arms and ran her toward the empty, moonlit beach.

The bulky cliffs that lined the shore loomed just ahead. Several large caves were burrowed into the rock—black, yawning mouths that had once been part of an ancient Roman emperor's crumbled stone villa that was a thousand years in ruin. Lazaro carried Melena inside one of the caves, past a littering of rough rocks and pools of tidal water, to a spot where the sand was soft and dry underfoot.

As he set her down, he couldn't help revisiting the night he'd carried a lifeless little girl into his Darkhaven in Boston. He'd remembered every minute of it, despite the indifference he'd feigned with Melena earlier on the yacht. She had been a seven-year-old child that first, and last, time he saw her before tonight. Back then, she had been as helpless and fragile as a baby bird to his mind. He'd rescued her the same way he would have done for any innocent child.

But now...

Now, Melena Walsh was a grown woman. She was as enticing a woman as he'd ever seen—even more so, with her lovely face and thick red hair, and all of her soft, feminine curves that drew his eye even as he carefully arranged her unresponsive, alarmingly chilled body on the sand.

And as fiercely as he'd wanted to save her life in Boston, he wanted to save her now.

Not the least of his reasons being his need to know what secret she was keeping from him. She'd been on the verge of telling him in the seconds before the yacht was blown to pieces. If that secret had anything to do with the attack tonight, he was going to see that Melena answered for it.

Lazaro felt in his bones that Opus Nostrum was behind the brazen act. Whoever did it knew just who and where to strike. But how did they know? Both parties were meticulously screened by the Order. Lazaro had personally vetted everyone in attendance, right down to the last man on the vessel's crew tonight. He'd approved them all.

Except Melena Walsh.

He gazed at her in the cave's darkness, his Breed eyes seeing her as clearly as if it were midday. She was beautiful, stunningly so. She was poised, intelligent, erudite. And he'd seen her wield her charm without effort over Turati and the rest of the men at the meeting.

Lazaro couldn't deny he'd been equally affected. More than affected, despite his unwillingness to give it reins. A woman like Melena would make a deadly asset, if allied with the wrong people.

He didn't want to think she might be his enemy, intentional or otherwise.

The fact that she'd nearly gotten killed tonight along with everyone else made it impossible to imagine her presence on the yacht could have had anything to do with the catastrophe that followed.

She would give him the truth, but first he had to make sure she stayed alive to do so.

Lazaro scowled at her sodden, bruised condition. Her skirt was shredded, her shoes lost like his somewhere between the yacht and the shore. Her blouse was in tatters, the burgundy colored silk dark with seawater...and blood. Fortunately, most of it was his.

Her hair drooped lifelessly into her face. Lazaro smoothed away some of the drenched red tangles, letting out a low curse when he saw how white her skin was. Her lips were slack, turned an alarming shade of blue. She had contusions on her forehead and chin. Blood from a scalp wound trailed in a bright red rivulet down her temple.

Fuck.

His vision honed in on that thin scarlet ribbon, everything Breed in him responding with keen, inhuman interest. The fact that she was a Breedmate made her blood an exponentially greater temptation to one of his kind.

Melena's blood carried the subtle fragrance of caramel and something sweeter still...dark cherries, Lazaro decided, his lungs soaking in a deeper breath even though it was torment to his senses.

His fangs punched out of his gums, throbbing against the firmly closed line of his lips. His vision sharpened some more, his irises throwing off a rising amber glow that bathed her paleness in warmer light. His own skin prickled with the sudden surge of heat in his veins.

If Melena opened her eyes now, she'd see him fully transformed to the bloodthirsty, otherworldly being he truly was.

If she opened her pretty, bright green eyes, she would know that his desire for her didn't stop at just her blood. He didn't want to think what kind of base creature he was that he could feel lust and hunger for a bruised, bloodied woman who'd just lost her father and nearly her own life too.

The truth was, he'd felt these same urges back on the yacht too. He hadn't wanted to admit it then either.

For all he knew, she could belong to another Breed male. Hell, she could already be blood-bonded to someone, a thought that should've relieved him rather than put a rankle in his brow. It would be pointless to let himself wonder, then or now. He wasn't about to act on either of his unwanted needs. Least of all with a woman bearing the Breedmate mark.

Since Ellie's death, he'd found other women to service him when required. Humans who understood the limits of his interest. More importantly, humans he could feed from without the shackle of a blood bond.

Instead here he was, shackled to the rescue and safekeeping of a woman he didn't fully trust and had no right to desire.

On a rough curse, ignoring the pounding demands of his veins, he stripped off his ragged black combat shirt and hunkered down in the sand alongside Melena. She moaned softly as he wrapped his arms around her. Her raspy sigh as she instinctively settled into his heat was an added torment he sure as hell didn't need.

Jaw clamped tight, pulse hammering with thinly bridled hunger, Lazaro gathered Melena to his naked chest to give her body the warmth it needed.

CHAPTER 4

She woke from an endless, cold nightmare, a scream lodged in her throat. She couldn't force out any sound, and when she dragged in a sudden gasp of air, her lungs felt shredded in her breast.

No, not her lungs.

Her heart.

All at once, the details flew back at her. The explosion. The fire and debris. The cold, black water.

Her father...

No, he couldn't be gone. Her kind and decent father—that strong Breed male—could not have been wiped from existence tonight.

Betrayed, murdered. Just as he'd feared.

Her father was dead.

Some rational part of her knew there was no other possibility, but accepting it hurt too much.

She tried to move and found herself trapped in a cocoon of warmth. Thick arms encircled her. Arms covered in Breed *dermaglpyhs.* The elaborate pattern of skin markings could only belong to one man.

"You're all right, Melena." Lazaro's deep voice rumbled against her ear. "Lie still. You need rest."

She felt him breathing, felt his large body's heat all around her. And God, she needed that heat and reassurance. Every particle of her being wanted to burrow deeper and just close her eyes and sleep. Try to forget...

But her father was out there in the dark. Left behind in the frigid water, while she was safe and protected in the shelter of Lazaro's arms.

She opened her eyes and took in her surroundings as best she could in the lightless space around them. She smelled the sea and wet rock. Felt soft sand beneath her.

"Where are we?" Her words came out like a croak. She swallowed past the salt and soot, attempted to extricate herself from the comfort she couldn't enjoy. She ached all over. Could barely summon strength to move her limbs.

"I brought you to Anzio. We're in a cave at Nero's villa ruins."

She had no idea where that was, only that it had to be a good long distance away from the yacht. "How long have we been here?"

"A few hours."

An irrational panic crushed down on her. "Why did you let me sleep for so long? We should be out there, searching for them!"

His answering curse vibrated against her spine. "Melena—"

"I have to get up. We have to go back for him, Lazaro. For all of them."

On a burst of adrenaline, she managed to slip out of his loose embrace. She sat up, registering dimly that her clothing was damp and ruined, torn open in more places than it was held together.

And Lazaro was only half-dressed. Just his black pants, clinging to him in tatters as well. No shirt on his bare, *glyph-* covered chest and muscled arms. There were numerous bruises on his torso and shoulders. When he sat up too, she noted that a healing gash in his thigh had bled through the material of his pants.

"There's no reason to go back, Melena. There's no chance of survivors."

She didn't want to hear him confirm the terror churning inside her. "No. You're wrong!" She made a clumsy falter to her feet. Lazaro stood with her, catching her by the arms before her sluggish legs could buckle beneath her. She didn't have the strength to break out of his hold again. "You *have* to be wrong. I have to go back and find him. My father—"

Lazaro shook his head. His handsome face was grim with sympathy and something darker. "I'm sorry, Melena. The missile strike was a direct hit. There was nothing left."

Some of her hysteria leaked out of her under his grave stare. She couldn't hold back the grief, the tears. It all flooded out of her on an ugly, shuddering sob. And then her knees did give out, and she sank back down to the sandy floor of the cave.

Lazaro's warm hands were still clasped on her arms as he crouched down in front of her. She couldn't stop the wracking anguish, no more than she could keep herself from pitching forward into his arms, clinging to him as she wept.

He held her there, for how long, she didn't know.

She only knew that after she didn't think she could cry anymore, or hurt any worse, he was still holding her. Still keeping her upright when the rest of her world was crumbling all around her.

"Why?" she murmured into his bulky shoulder. "My God, he knew this. He was so afraid he was going to die soon. Who would do this to him? Why?"

Lazaro gently pulled her away from him, his ebony brows knit in a tight scowl. "Your father feared for his life?" Confusion flashed across his features, then settled into suspicion. "Damn it. Why didn't he tell me this? We spoke several times before the meeting. He had plenty of opportunity to say something if he felt he was in danger in any way."

Melena shook her head, heartsick. "He didn't know who he could trust. He'd been having premonitions, sensing some kind of betrayal. He knew he was going to die soon. He didn't know when, or where the betrayal would come from. He wasn't sure of anyone anymore."

"Not even me," Lazaro replied. "Jesus Christ, why didn't he cancel the damned meeting? He could have made any excuse."

"I told him the same thing. But it was too important to him. And he didn't know what would happen tonight. Neither one of us knew." She thought back on the time she and her father spent with Paolo Turati. She had detected no hidden agendas. No duplicity or harmful intent in any one of them.

Lazaro was studying her in unreadable silence. "You need to tell me the truth, Melena. Beginning with why your father brought you with him tonight."

She gave him a weak nod. There was no more reason for her to keep it from him. Her father was gone. He had nothing left to lose if word of his paranoia became public. Melena no longer needed to protect him. "I've been traveling with him everywhere for months now. He can't bear to go—he *couldn't* bear," she corrected herself quietly, "to go anywhere unless I was there to assure him no one meant him any harm."

"How so?"

"You were right that it wasn't only my translation skills that brought me here tonight. It was my ability to see people's auras. I can tell at a glance if someone's intentions are good or not."

"Your Breedmate talent," Lazaro murmured. There seemed to be a trace of relief in his tone. "So, when you looked at Turati and the others on the yacht tonight?"

She shook her head. "There was nothing to fear from any of them."

"Did your father voice his concerns to any of his colleagues in the GNC?"

"No."

"Anyone outside the Council?"

"No one," she replied, certain of it.

Lazaro grunted, and she could see his gaze go distant as his mind began to churn on the information. She knew he and the Order would not let this attack go unmet, and there was a vengeful part of her that longed to see the guilty tortured to within an inch of their sadistic, cowardly lives.

"Make them pay, Lazaro."

"They will," he answered solemnly. "Whoever had a hand in this, they will be found. There will be justice."

Her tears started up again, but they were quieter now, filled with more rage and resolve than bereavement. She hadn't been prepared for Lazaro's tender touch. She held her breath as he caught her chin on the edge of his fingertips and lifted her gaze to his. He stroked her cheek, his thumb sweeping away the wet trail of her tears.

She could sense his tenderness went deeper than mere concern.

She could see the evidence of that truth in the crackling sparks of amber that were lighting in the deep sapphire of his irises. She could see it in his *dermaglyphs*, which surged with dark colors across every muscled inch of his torso and arms, the intriguing swirls and arcs of the *glyphs'* pattern changing hues before her eyes.

And if all of that weren't enough, she could see his intent in his aura, which formed a smoldering glow around him now, confirming the astonishing fact.

Lazaro Archer wanted her.

No sooner had the thought entered her mind than he leaned down and brushed his lips over hers. Her breath was already shaky and thin, but as his mouth pressed against hers, her lungs dried up on a slow moan. The kiss was tender, careful, no doubt meant to console or soothe her.

It did both, but it also inflamed her.

Heat raced through her at the feel of his mouth on hers. She didn't want to feel it—not now, not when her heart was breaking over the loss of her father and fear still held her in a firm grasp.

But Lazaro's arms were stronger than any of that. His gentling, but arousing, kiss made her melt against him with a desire she could hardly reconcile.

And he broke away much too soon for her liking.

His Breed pupils had narrowed to the thinnest vertical slits. And when he ground out a vivid curse, the tips of his fangs gleamed white and razor-sharp.

"Fuck." He let go of her. "That shouldn't have happened. I apologize."

"Don't," she murmured, her voice a raspy whisper. Desire was singing through her veins—uninvited, maybe, but too powerful to be denied. "I didn't mind, Lazaro. I...liked it."

"Christ, don't say that." He blew out a harsh breath, then drew back from her as though she had scorched him too, and not in the good way he'd ignited her. "You do not want to say that to me, Melena. For the good of both of us."

He got to his feet in abrupt, stony silence. As he stood, she noticed that the gash in his thigh was still bleeding. While he'd been looking after her these past few hours, he'd neglected his own injuries. He seemed oblivious to it, walking over to examine a comm unit that lay on a nearby rock. He shook the device, swearing as water dripped out of it.

"That wound on your leg needs attention, Lazaro." He was Breed, Gen One besides. She knew his body would heal itself, but even a vampire needed help sometimes. "You need to feed soon."

"Is that an invitation, Miss Walsh?" The comm unit clutched in his fist, he snarled down at her, baring his teeth and fangs. God, they were huge. Terrifying, and he damned well knew it. His aura seethed as menacingly as the rest of him. When she shrank back a little where she sat, he gave a dark chuckle. "No, I didn't think so. Smart girl. Do us both a favor and don't concern yourself with what I need."

His anger confused her, almost as much as his unexpected tenderness of a moment ago. And the fact that he wanted to push her away when he was the only reason she was alive right now kind of pissed her off too. She stood up, refusing to be cowed by his bluster.

"Why shouldn't I be concerned? You just saved my life— for the second time, in fact. So, forgive me if that makes me care about you just a little bit."

When he scoffed and took a long stride away from her, she followed after him. When she put her hand on his shoulder, he rounded on her with a hiss. "Just because you're alive, doesn't mean you're safe with me. Don't make the mistake of thinking I'm some kind of hero."

He didn't give her the opportunity to reply. On a furious

glower, he pivoted to stalk toward the mouth of the cave. "Stay put. I'm going to see about sending a signal and getting us out of here."

Melena watched him prowl out into the darkness, his kiss still warming her lips and his harsh words ringing in her ears.

Don't make the mistake of thinking I'm some kind of hero.

Didn't he know? She'd been thinking of him that way for most of her life.

CHAPTER 5

One of Lazaro's comrades showed up less than an hour later to retrieve them in a big black SUV. Melena had hardly been introduced to the Breed warrior who drove them—a towering male with a mass of loose golden curls and a dimpled, quicksilver smile that instantly softened his strong, square-cut jaw. She thought he'd said his name was Savage, but in her opinion, he looked more like a fallen angel. If fallen angels wore combat patrol gear and bristled with blades and heavy firearms.

The warrior seemed already aware of who she was and how she'd come to be in his Order commander's company, although he didn't so much as try to ask. It was obvious from Lazaro's menacing silence during the ride to wherever they were heading that conversation with her was neither welcomed nor encouraged.

Where they'd been heading was Rome.

More specifically, the Order's command center in that city.

Melena tried not to gape when she realized that's where Lazaro had brought her. Neither the late-night sight of the illuminated Colosseum nor Pantheon had inspired more than a lingering look as they passed the monuments, but when the SUV approached a gated, secured mansion compound nestled in the heart of the sprawling city, Melena couldn't help but sit up a little straighter in her seat and draw in her breath.

The stately white brick mansion with its elegant, carved marble detailing and old bronze fixtures looked as timeless as the city around it. But it didn't take long to understand that the structure's antiquity ended at the street. This was a modern fortress, beautiful and sturdy and impenetrable. Inside the massive gates, motion sensors followed the SUV's progress toward an underground parking garage around back.

Once they got out of the vehicle, Lazaro sternly instructed her to follow him. The warrior who drove them lingered behind, leaving her alone to his commander's dubious care.

Lazaro took her not into the living quarters of the compound, but to another wing of the estate that seemed to be where the warriors conducted Order business. She heard two male voices in one of the rooms they passed along the corridor, but her escort didn't slow his pace at all.

Actually, it didn't seem that he could get rid of her fast enough for his liking.

A few minutes later, Melena found herself abandoned to a vaguely medical-seeming room. The small space contained the hard bed she sat upon, and next to it a single chair. Glass-fronted cupboards mounted to the wall opposite her appeared to house bandages and other field dressing supplies.

She wasn't sure how long she sat there, feeling awkward and unwanted in Lazaro's domain. At some point, she dozed, still exhausted from her ordeal and the raw grief that clung to her. A couple of times, she'd glanced toward the window in the infirmary room door and saw one of the warriors stride past.

The gorgeous blond who brought her there had smiled through the glass as he walked by. Another Breed male, a mean-looking warrior with a shaved head and a jagged facial scar that made him more suited to the name "Savage" than his friendly comrade, spared her only the briefest, disinterested glance.

But it was a different warrior altogether who finally came into the room. Hulking and immense, he had a mane of shoulder-length brown waves and skin the color of sun-kissed golden sand. Arresting sky-blue eyes scrutinized her from within his ruggedly handsome, exotic face. "Melena. How are you feeling?" As big and imposing as the Breed male was, he somehow moved with the easy, feline grace of a jungle cat as he approached. His voice was rich and deep and cultured. "I am Jehan."

"Nice to meet you," she replied, her manners on automatic pilot.

"Commander Archer sent me to see if your injuries need tending. I must apologize that we're not equipped for treating wounds outside of the Breed, but I can get you medicine for your pain. There are ointments I can prepare to make the contusions heal faster."

Melena shook her head. "Thank you, but no." Compared to the pain of her grief and fear following the attack, and the lingering exhaustion from what she suspected had been hypothermia back in the cave, her assortment of cuts and bruises were a minor issue. "I'm okay."

He eyed her skeptically, folding his *glyph*-covered muscled arms over his chest. "You've endured quite an ordeal. You're certain there is nothing you need?"

Melena gave a vague shrug. She wasn't certain of anything at the moment. Part of her wanted to bolt for the door and find the fastest way out of this nightmare, back home to Maryland.

Another part of her just wanted to crawl under the covers of the bed and scream.

"I know this can't be easy," Jehan said, genuine concern in his low voice. "And I am sorry for your loss."

"Thank you." Although she was well-versed in multiple languages, she couldn't quite place his unusual accent. His name was old French, if she wasn't mistaken, but the formal way he carried himself and the way he spoke had her curious. "Where are you from, Jehan?"

"All around," he answered cryptically. "But it's Morocco you hear in my voice. My father's homeland."

That explained it. He had the kind of voice that made her imagine moonlit desert plains and the spicy fragrance of incense and woodsmoke. "Your mother wasn't Moroccan, though?"

"Born and raised in Paris," he confirmed, his sensual mouth curving at the corners. "She and my father met in France. After they were mated, he brought her back with him to our tribe's Darkhaven in his country."

"Your tribe?"

Jehan's dark brows quirked. "A relic of a term." He shrugged it off, but something mysterious flickered in his mesmerizing gaze. "My father's Breed line is very old. Its roots go deep into Moroccan soil. Burrowed in almost as stubbornly as the old man's heels."

"What about you?" Melena asked, genuinely curious.

Jehan inclined his head, almost courtly in its tilt. "To my father's eternal regret, his eldest son's feet refused to stay put. Despite the shackle of obligation he's tried to affix to them."

As they spoke, the door opened again and the blond warrior came in. He grinned, his hazel eyes bouncing off Jehan for a second before fixing on Melena. "I see Prince Jehan is already trying to dazzle you with his long, boring pedigree."

Melena swung a questioning look on the enigmatic warrior. "Prince?"

Jehan grunted under his breath, but didn't deny it. "What are you doing here, Sav? You know damned well Lazaro's orders were that no one enter this room or speak to Melena without his permission."

Melena wanted to be offended by the news of that domineering command, but her two visitors were a welcome distraction from everything else going on. Not the least of which being Lazaro Archer's stinging rejection of her in the cave. A sting that hurt all the worse for his tenderness when he touched her...kissed her.

"We weren't properly introduced," Sav said. "Ettore Roberto Selvaggio."

His dimples deepened along with his heart-stopping smile. His Italian accent seemed to deepen as well, the kind of accent that probably ensured he never wanted for female company.

"Melena Walsh," she replied. "I thought I heard Lazaro call you Savage."

"Lazaro?" he echoed.

She felt color rise to her cheeks. "Your commander. Mr. Archer. Whatever I should call him," she muttered. The man who saved her life, awoke an irresistible desire in her, but made her feel as if he might have rather left her behind in Anzio a few hours ago. "I think he despises me."

The two Breed males now exchanged a look. Jehan was the first to talk. "Don't let him scare you. It's just his way."

"Come on, man," his comrade said. "It goes a bit deeper than that."

Melena glanced at them both. "What do you mean?"

"The way I heard it, Archer's never been the same since he lost his family back in Boston twenty years ago," Sav said. "He blames himself, I imagine."

"Why would he do that?" She couldn't begin to guess how Lazaro could hold himself even the least responsible for what happened to his kin. "The Darkhaven was attacked while he wasn't home. It was razed to the ground."

"Yes," Jehan agreed soberly. "And now imagine you have the incredible gift of walking into even the most extreme temperature and emerging wholly unscathed. But you're not there when the attack on your own loved ones takes place."

"You have the ability to save some of them—maybe all of them," Sav added. "Instead, you lose them all in one fell swoop."

Melena couldn't speak. She wasn't even sure she was breathing as the weight of what she'd just heard settled on her.

She hadn't known about Lazaro's Breed gift. Now it made sense, of course. His ability to search for her for so long in the frozen pond all those years ago. The fact that he'd swum across nearly half of the Tyrrhenian Sea to save her tonight, impervious to the cold, unlike her.

He'd saved her twice, but had been unable to save the ones he loved. Including his blood-bonded Breedmate.

"He will not be pleased if he knew we told you," Jehan warned grimly.

Sav gave a nod. "Probably want to stake both of us out in the sun. Or worse." He glanced at Melena. "So, not a word, yeah?"

"Okay," she murmured woodenly. But oh, God, her heart ached for Lazaro now.

"Enough about him," Sav said, grinning as if he wanted to lighten the grave mood. "You asked about me, if I recall. So, to answer your question, yes. Most people who know me call me Savage."

She took his bait, needing to put her sympathy for Lazaro on a higher shelf. He wouldn't want it anyway. "Why do they call you that? You seem nice enough to me. Are you usually mean or something?"

"Or something," he said, the glint in his eye and the playful, seductive hue of his aura providing all the correction she needed.

Jehan snorted. "He's a legend in his own mind. Pay no attention to him."

Sav barked a laugh. "Envy isn't a good look for you, Highness."

"And you may kiss my royal ass, peasant."

Melena found herself smiling with them. She took in their banter and warm, welcoming faces, not realizing until then how much she needed to feel she was among friends.

She needed her family, which was now reduced to just one other person. Her Breed brother, Derek, had been living in Paris for the past year, bouncing between England and France on one business venture or another.

Melena hadn't seen him since he left, hadn't even spoken to him for several long weeks. She couldn't imagine the anguish it would cause him to learn their father had been killed. Before he heard it anywhere else, she wanted to be the one to break the news to him. She wanted to spare him the unnecessary grief of thinking she had died along with everyone else tonight.

"Do you think it would be possible for me to try to reach my brother somehow?" she asked the two warriors. "He's traveling and I need to let him know—"

"Is there a reason half my team is not where I expect them to be?" Lazaro's deep, furious growl interrupted the conversation without warning. He stood in the open doorway, looking every bit as ferocious as a Gen One Breed male could.

His sapphire eyes were thunderously dark, except for the flashes of amber outrage sparking in their depths. "Out. Both of you. Now."

Sav and Jehan departed on command.

Leaving Melena to face Lazaro's rage by herself.

She waited for him to lay into her too, but he didn't. He merely stared at her, a tendon ticking hard in his jaw. His aura was as stormy as his glower, back to the gunmetal haze that she found so difficult to read.

His animosity seemed clear enough. He didn't want her in his command center any more than he'd wanted her in his presence on the yacht or at the cave.

And she wanted to be somewhere safe now, even if that meant returning to her father's empty Darkhaven in the States. "I don't want to be here," she murmured. "I need to get in touch with my brother Derek, and I need to go home."

"Out of the question." His answer was firm, flat. Unyielding. "I've spoken to Lucan Thorne. Before you go anywhere else, he wants me to bring you to the Order's headquarters in Washington, D.C. He'll talk with you there, debrief you."

"I already told you everything I know. What more can I tell him?"

Lazaro didn't answer. "We leave tomorrow evening, Melena." He started to go, then pivoted back to her. "In the meantime, I won't have my team distracted by the fact we have a Breedmate underfoot. I'll make a place for you in the villa. You'll stay there until we depart for D.C."

CHAPTER 6

Melena had been moved out of the command center's infirmary to the living quarters of the mansion hours ago. Lazaro's team had gone back to their business as instructed. The morning passed with discussions of Order objectives and priorities. Chief among those priorities being to ensure that reports of the tragic, "accidental" explosion on board Paolo Turati's yacht didn't brush up against the truth that it was, in fact, a stealth missile attack.

And while no one yet had stepped forward to publicly claim responsibility, there wasn't a shred of doubt among the Order's entire organization that the killings were surely instigated by Opus Nostrum.

Halfway through the afternoon in Rome, the warriors were now dispersed to prepare for their patrols that coming evening, everyone focused on task and ready to carry out their missions.

And yet the female under their roof remained a distraction.

For Lazaro, that is.

He made his way through the corridors in a foul mood. He

didn't want to think about her. He didn't want to think about his irritation over finding Sav and Jehan chatting her up earlier, making her smile in spite of everything she'd been through. He didn't want to think about the anger that had shot through him in that moment—the blast of pure male possessiveness that he had no right to feel.

And he sure as hell did not want to give another moment's thought to the kiss he stole from Melena back in the Anzio cave. He'd had no right to take that liberty either. But was the kiss truly stolen if she didn't seem to mind that he did it?

She'd told him she enjoyed it, for fuck's sake.

His blood rushed a bit faster, disturbingly hotter, at just the thought. And a lot of that blood was making a swift run south. It pounded through his veins like liquid fire, settling in his groin when he recalled how soft and inviting her mouth had been under his.

Melena had more than liked his kiss. She'd welcomed it. Wanted more.

Wanted him.

Christ, he couldn't get away from her fast enough after that kiss. He still couldn't put enough distance between them for his peace of mind. How he was going to manage the long hours between now and their departure for D.C. tomorrow evening, he had no damned idea.

More than likely, he'd be spending that stretch of time with a constant hard-on and a fevered hunger that bordered on madness. He needed to exorcise that hunger, and soon. He was on his way to the weapons room to sweat out some of his aggression with his blades and pistols when one of his men met him in the corridor.

Trygg had been the only one of the unit with sense enough to avoid their pretty, uninvited guest. The bald, menacing looking Breed male carried a long, cream-colored box in his arms. "Package you ordered this morning just arrived."

Lazaro grunted as he took the box from the most intimidating member of his team.

"You want me to deliver it to her?" Trygg suggested.

"No." The reply came out too quickly, too forcefully, but there it was. Melena had been through enough of a scare already; she didn't need a brutal killer like Trygg showing up at her door, even if he did it with an unlikely gift in his hands.

Besides, Lazaro had placed the order for her as something more than just a courtesy. He supposed he'd been hoping it would also serve as some kind of apology. He'd been a warrior for twenty years, but he liked to think there was still some sense of decency in him. Given the way he'd treated Melena so far, she might be hard-pressed to agree.

"I'll bring it myself," he told Trygg. The vampire merely stared, his shrewd eyes unblinking, far too knowing. Lazaro tucked the long box under his arm. "There is something you can do. Locate Derek Walsh. Melena said her brother's been spending his time between Paris and the United Kingdom. When you've got a bead on him, let me know."

Trygg gave a slight nod. "Done."

Lazaro stalked through the command center to the attached, four-story residential quarters. The Roman villa had ten bedrooms, but Melena had been placed in the largest suite in the estate. It was also the one place where he knew neither of her newest admirers would be tempted to seek her out.

Paused outside the closed door of his private quarters on the top floor, Lazaro noted she'd left the tray of food he'd delivered hours earlier untouched. It didn't appear she'd even come out to look at it.

He listened for movement on the other side. Hearing

nothing, he rapped his knuckles on the carved wooden door. He waited, feeling both awkward and annoyed.

When he knocked again and got no response, he started to get concerned.

He opened the door and peered inside. "Melena?"

His suite spanned the entirety of the villa's fourth floor. He didn't see her anywhere, not even in the spacious bedroom. He dropped the box on the end of the king-sized bed, then noticed the door to the en suite bath was cracked open.

Through the thin wedge, he saw her slip into a terry robe, apparently having just stepped out of the tub. He caught an unexpected glimpse of her bare skin—delectable curves, lovely breasts peaked with dusky peach nipples...the hint of dark curls at the *V* of her creamy thighs.

Ah, damn, she was gorgeous.

Everything male in him responded as swiftly—and as obviously—as everything Breed in him. His pulse jackhammered, the drum filling his ears with a rush of hot need. The tips of his fangs dug into his tongue, and as he stared at her, his gaze grew heated as his pupils thinned with his hunger and his cock thickened with desire.

Until he spotted the bruises that still lingered on her. His own wounds had healed, thanks to his Gen One metabolism, but Melena still carried numerous contusions on her ribs and delicate belly.

"Fuck." Lazaro's growled reaction made her look up sharply. Too late to pivot around and leave. Too late to pretend he hadn't just crept into the room and stood there ogling her in open lust. Or to hope she wouldn't notice how powerfully she affected him.

Her expression was guarded, wary. She opened the door wider, but he noticed how tightly she now gripped the edges of the robe at her chest. When Lazaro took a step toward her, she slipped out of the bathroom and into the larger space of the bedroom.

With some effort, he curbed the presence of his fangs. His vision was still awash in amber, but he could feel his pupils resuming a less feral state. And as for the state of his arousal, that was a more difficult thing to hide, let alone suppress. But while his body was still thrumming with awareness—and want—of her, his primary interest in that moment was Melena's well being.

"Jehan was supposed to look after your injuries when you arrived," he muttered angrily. "He's skilled with ointments and herbs. He should've given you something to help you heal."

"I told Jehan I was fine. And I am...or at least, I can try to be, once you and the Order allow me to go home."

Lazaro ignored the pointed complaint, even if it had merit. "I see you didn't eat anything either."

"What do you care?" she tossed back, her fine auburn brows pinched together.

"I care, Melena. For now, you're under my watch. It's my responsibility to ensure that you're comfortable and healthy. That you're fed and clothed." He gestured toward the boutique box on the bed. "I arranged for some things to be sent here for you from one of the local shops."

She cast a sidelong glance toward his gift, then back toward the bathroom where her ruined skirt and blouse lay in rags on the tile floor. Warily, she drifted over to the bed and lifted the lid off the box. She glanced inside, then one by one, pulled out the skirt and pants, then the blouse and sweater he selected for her.

"I didn't know what you'd prefer," he murmured.

She lifted the charcoal gray, fine-gauge sweater first, then the pair of black slacks. The understated classics of the collection, which didn't surprise him. She glanced at the two pairs of shoes he'd purchased as well, taking out the elegant Italian flats. "These are all in my sizes. Perfectly in my sizes." She slanted him a guarded look. "I wouldn't think you'd paid attention long enough to notice."

"I noticed." Lazaro slowly approached her near the bed. "I should be focused on a thousand other things right now. Instead, here I am. Noticing everything about you, Melena."

If she had flinched at all when he came to stand beside her, Lazaro would have somehow found the strength of will to leave her in peace.

If she had resisted even a little when he lifted her chin on his fingertips and drew her gaze up to his—if she had looked into his transformed Breed eyes with anything close to fear or uncertainty—he would have forced himself to let go of her and refrain from ever touching her again.

But Melena did none of those things.

And when he slowly lowered his mouth to hers, this time, not even he or his iron will could pretend the desire that arced between them was anything either of them would be able to deny.

He kissed her, hard and hungry. Any illusions he might have had for taking things slowly with her, or giving her a chance to get away before he pounced, were all but obliterated once their lips and tongues had come together.

A fresh surge of molten need scorched through his veins, and all at once it didn't matter to him that getting involved with Melena Walsh was the last thing he needed to be doing.

He wanted her.

She wanted him—he knew that even in the cave.

And the fact was, he'd already let himself get involved,

whether or not they allowed this undeniable, if untimely, desire for each other to flare any further out of control.

Melena awakened a need in him that he hadn't felt in a long time. A new kind of need, something white-hot and irresistible. She had done in less than a day what no other woman before her had managed to do in two decades.

She made him feel alive again.

Lazaro growled and took her mouth in a deeper kiss. She moaned, reaching up to burrow her fingers into the short hair at his nape. Her soft curves felt like heaven against him, even through the barrier of their clothing. Her mouth tasted warm and sweet. Her body arched into his, pliant, consenting.

Welcoming.

Hot with need.

He smoothed his hand down her throat, breaking their kiss as his thumb grazed over the Breedmate mark nestled in the hollow between her collarbones. He lifted his head to look at it—to remind himself of what she was and why he could not allow himself anything more than this desire they shared.

"I should ask you if there is someone else," he uttered thickly. He dragged his smoldering gaze back up to hers. "I should ask, but right now I don't think I'll give a damn if you say there is."

"No." She gave a faint shake of her head, her breast rising and falling with each rapid pant of her breath. "There's no one. Not for more than a year. And even then, I never wanted anyone like this..."

He registered that sweet confession with a growl that vibrated deep in his chest.

He kissed her again, gathering her face in his hands while his mouth moved intensely, hungrily, over hers. Being Gen One, his appetites were stronger than most. With Melena all but undressed and willing in his arms, those appetites were on the verge of owning him. It was only the dim knowledge of her lingering injuries that kept him in check.

And she wasn't helping in that regard.

Meeting each thrust of his tongue, parting her lips to take him deeper, she stoked his arousal even further. Her body pressed against his, heat igniting everywhere they touched. He couldn't resist the loosened opening of her robe. His hand slipped inside to feel the softness of her skin. Her pulse banged against his fingertips, strong and certain. Erotic and primal.

Melena groaned in pleasure. Her voice rasped sensually against his mouth. "I like the way you kiss me, Lazaro. I like the way you touch me."

Holy hell. Her words made fire erupt in his already molten blood.

With fangs filling his mouth and his cock gone hard as granite behind the zipper of his pants, Lazaro moved his hand to cup the buoyant underside of her breast. A hot, pent-up sigh gusted out of her as he caressed her bare skin beneath the slackened robe. Her nipple was pebbled and erect, a temptation he lightly tweaked, then rolled between his fingers. Melena's grasp at the back of his neck tightened, her fingers curling into his hair as a moan leaked through her parted lips.

Every taut fiber of his being ached with the need to put his mouth on her silken skin, to feel all of her. Taste all of her.

His hands obeyed that need, reaching up to gently ease the robe off Melena's shoulders. It slipped down her arms, baring her to the waist. She was so lovely. Porcelain skin dusted with a smattering of sweet, peachy freckles and lush, feminine curves that begged to be savored.

The purple contusions and mending cuts on her torso and abdomen drew his eye just as intensely. Rage for whoever did it swirled through him like a fierce tempest. When he thought of how close she'd come to being lost in the explosion along with everyone else, that rage turned murderous and black.

But tenderly, he let his fingers light on a couple of her worst bruises. She flinched a little and some of his fury snarled out of him. "It hurts?"

"Only a bit." When he drew his hand away, she caught it, placed his palm atop her bare breast. "I don't want you to stop touching me."

His cock jerked in response, more than eager for him to oblige her. He filled his hand with her breast, then took her mouth in another deep kiss.

But feeling her, kissing her, only made him ache to explore some more.

His entire Gen One being throbbed with the need to claim, to possess.

He drew the robe off her completely. Let it fall in a pool at her feet. For one indulgent moment, he soaked in the sight of her through his amber-drenched, fevered eyes.

Then he lifted her off her feet and spread her out beneath him on his bed.

CHAPTER 7

Melena sank down onto the soft mattress and watched, wide-eyed and trembling, as Lazaro prowled up the length of her naked body.

It wasn't fear that gripped her. Nothing even close to fear.

Her every nerve ending had come alive—gone dizzyingly electric—under his careful, caressing touch and the sensual promise of his lips and tongue as he'd tenderly explored her skin.

Now, lying exposed to him completely on the bed while he remained clothed, she wasn't uncomfortable in the least. And whether that made her a wanton harlot or a daring fool, she didn't know. Nor did she care in that moment.

She wasn't nervous or uncertain about anything she was doing with this man.

She wanted more.

He sent the boutique box to the floor with a sweep of his strong arm, making more room for them. She jumped, breath catching at the animalistic power that poured off Lazaro in palpable waves. She'd never felt so much energy and heat focused on her.

In her handful of failed relationships, no other man—Breed or human—had stirred her passion so easily, so masterfully. *Difficult to please*, more than one lover had called her. And they'd been right. None of them had taken her breath away. None of them had been able to hold her interest, in or out of bed, for more than a few months.

Then again, they weren't Lazaro Archer.

She'd never been in the presence of a Gen One male with carnal hunger in his eyes.

And Lazaro's hunger was intense.

His eyes were twin coals, locked on her as he positioned himself above her, braced on his strong fists on either side of her head. His fangs gleamed razor-sharp, enormous and fully extended.

And while his *dermaglyphs* were obscured by his black shirt and combat pants, she knew they had to be vivid with deep colors—not unlike the pulsating, blood-red aura that radiated from him as his consuming gaze drank in her nakedness from forehead to ankle.

He spread her legs with his thigh, nudging her open to him. As he covered her, the rigid length of his arousal ground against her hip. Her pulse sped up, tripping as he gave her a meaningful thrust of his pelvis, those smoldering amber irises burning her up.

He took her mouth in a slow but demanding kiss. He took her lip between his teeth, sucked her tongue deep into his mouth. Kissed her until she was panting and writhing beneath him, grasping at him with needy hands. "Now, I'm going to taste you, Melena," he murmured against her slack mouth. "Every last creamy, delectable inch of you."

And then, heaven help her, he proceeded to do just that.

He started with a maddening sweep of his tongue just below her ear. She shivered, even though her blood was on fire for the heat of his lips and the gentle, but unmistakable, rasp of his fangs as he dragged his mouth down to the curve where her neck and shoulder met. He suckled and nipped, working his way to her breasts. Kneading them in strong hands, tonguing the tight buds at their peaks, he didn't move on until she was moaning with pleasure and aching for more.

Her back arched into him as he began a slow and steady exploration of her rib cage and abdomen. He took care around her bruises, astonishing tenderness from a Breed male who had lived ten lifetimes and counting, whose own otherworldly body was virtually indestructible. Yet he navigated her minor wounds as though he were handling glass.

That moved her deeply, even more than his passion had overwhelmed her.

Melena reached down, cradling his dark head in her hands while his kiss traveled lower.

Across her stomach, onto each hip bone, over the quivering tops of her thighs. She trembled as his mouth blazed a slow path down the entire length of her right leg and ankle, then returned up her left calf, to her knee and the tingling flesh of her inner thigh.

If he wanted to make her wet and vibrating with the need to have him inside her, Lazaro could have stopped right after their lips had met for the first time here in his bedroom.

But it was patently clear from the wicked look he shot up the length of her nude body that he was only getting started.

His head lowered between her spread legs. When the heat of his breath rushed out against her sex, she shuddered. When his lips touched down and his hot, silky tongue cleaved into her slit, she let out a strangled cry.

Fingers gripping the coverlet on each side of her, she held on for dear life as Lazaro licked and kissed and fucked her senseless with his ruthlessly skilled mouth.

She came in mere moments, pleasure shooting through her in wave after glorious wave. She didn't know if she sighed or screamed or both. She only knew that while her body was still floating in a million tiny shards of bliss, Lazaro started climbing back up to her on the bed.

He stroked her face, watching her—smirking in obvious satisfaction, for God's sake.

Then his grin was gone as quickly as it had arrived, and he covered her mouth with his, kissing her hard and deep and wild.

He drew back on a curse, his breath sawing in and out of his lungs. He stripped off his clothing and boots in mere seconds. Then he pivoted back to her, gloriously naked. He found his place between her thighs again and held himself there, unmoving, watching her. Considering her in some way.

His big body threw off waves of heat and power. The *glyphs* that traced his bulky shoulders and muscular arms continued onto the contours of his chest and rippled abdomen. They pulsed vividly on his skin, alive and flooded with color.

Those Gen One skin markings trekked farther south as well. The thick, long shaft of his cock was circled with *glyphs*, their hues flushing even deeper as Melena admired him with unabashed approval.

God, he was immense. Magnificently so.

And sexy as hell.

She rose up to touch his face, cupping his stern jaw in her palm when a scowl thundered across his expression. "It's been a while for me too," he said, then gave a small shake of his head. "I'm not sure I can be as gentle as I'd like for you. The last thing

I want to do is hurt you."

Melena saw the torment in his aura, even if his body was being driven by a stronger need now. He didn't want to let her in, but he couldn't shut her out either.

He cared, even though he wanted to deny it.

She thought back to what he said to her in the cave. That just because he'd helped her stay alive, didn't mean she was safe with him.

Melena had never felt more protected or secure with anyone in her life.

And she'd never known anything so raw and consuming— so impossible to deny—as how it felt being with Lazaro.

She wrapped her hand around his nape and pulled him down in a deep, scorching kiss. With her other hand, she sought out his cock and grasped it firmly, pumping his length in sure, steady strokes. She didn't let go of his mouth or his penis for a good long moment. When she did, she gave him a smile against his parted lips and the fangs that now filled his mouth even more than before. "See?" she told him. "I'm not going to break."

He uttered a low, vicious curse that sounded to be half relief and half anguish.

Then he positioned himself at her body's entrance and drove home, deep and slow and long, all the way to the hilt.

He filled her so completely she could hardly summon her breath. Then he started to pivot in and out, rolling his hips in controlled, tantalizing swivels that dragged a curse out of her too. Sweet pressure spiraled within her core as he pushed her toward another climax. He didn't go gently, instead driving into her so far and fully, it was all she could do to hold on to him and let her body shatter in his arms.

Lazaro watched her as she came, his eyes locked on hers.

She couldn't look away. The power of the connection was too intense. He felt it too—he had to have felt it.

As his own release built, then broke on a coarse shout, he kept his gaze fastened on hers too. It was so intense, so startlingly real, this thing coming to life between them.

If anything had the power to terrify her, it was this.

The feeling that she had already given herself to this man. A man who had pretended he barely remembered her when he first saw her on Turati's yacht.

A man who warned her not to get close to him, all but threatened that he would only hurt her.

And here she was, giving him her body.

Staring into his eyes as she surrendered the most intimate part of herself to him, and imagining that she could so easily let herself fall. That maybe she already had. Maybe the men in her past had been right. They would never have been good enough for her.

Because all along, what she wanted them to be was someone like Lazaro Archer. Brave. Loyal. And yes, heroic, even if he refused to accept that truth.

She didn't need him to be perfect, because even through the haze of affection and searing desire, she knew he would never be perfect. He didn't need to be. Not for her to want him like she did. Not for her to feel so right, so safe and contented in his arms.

Oh, God...could she be falling so fast?

Did she dare?

Melena finally broke his gaze then, turning her head away from him to the side, bewildered by her epiphany.

Her heart was pounding hard, making her carotid tick palpably in the side of her neck.

She didn't have to look back to him to know that Lazaro's

amber eyes had drifted to that fluttering vein. She felt the heat of his stare. Then she heard a dangerously low growl curl up from the back of his throat.

She went very still, terrified he might bite her.

Terrified he wouldn't.

"Lazaro?" she whispered, uncertain what she was about to ask him to do.

She slowly pivoted her head back to look at him and saw torment in his handsome, otherworldly face. And fury. He drew back from her on a hiss.

His expression was wild looking, intense...and his smoldering aura told her he was balanced on the razor's edge of a rigidly held, but tenuous, control.

* * * *

What the fuck was he doing?

Lazaro came to his senses as if physically struck. He was still buried inside Melena's hot, wet heat, his pulse still charged and racing. His cock was still hard, still greedy, even after the climax that had ripped through him with brutal ferocity.

And he'd been reckless enough to let his fevered gaze drift to the vein that throbbed so enticingly in the side of her vulnerable throat.

Christ.

He'd nearly lost control—something he never allowed to happen. Not once in twenty years had he even been tempted. His guard was always up, his will impenetrable.

Even then, he'd made a habit of avoiding women like Melena, females with the Breedmate mark. To drink from one of her kind would tie him to her singularly, irrevocably. He would always crave her. He would always feel her in his blood, in the root of his soul...unless death severed the bond, as it did when he lost Ellie.

Why the thought didn't freeze his thirst or shrivel his desire for Melena, he didn't want to know. And he sure as hell wasn't going to sit there pondering that fact as she gaped at him in mute terror.

"Damn it." He pulled out of her on a roar. As difficult as it was to deny himself the feel of her silken grip on his shaft—as much as he wanted to have her now, still, again and again—he needed the separation more.

What he needed was to put as much distance as possible between her soft, inviting body and the blood hunger that was suddenly twisting him in vicious knots.

He got off the bed to collect his clothes.

"What are you doing?" Melena asked from behind him. When he began to dress, he heard her slide across the sheets. "Talk to me, please."

He couldn't form words, let alone push them out of his mouth. He still wanted her too much, and he feared that if he let himself cave to that need now, he might not be able to reign it back in. He zipped up his pants, ignoring the persistent bulge of his uncooperative arousal. His hands moved hastily, aggressively, as he donned his shirt, then bent to retrieve his boots.

He had plenty of human females he could call upon to slake his needs. A pity he didn't think to do that before he made the mistake of putting himself alone in the company of a Breedmate as tempting as Melena.

And what a feeble fucking rationalization that was.

Nothing would satisfy him more than to dismiss his near-mistake as something that might have occurred with any female sporting the teardrop-and-crescent-moon birthmark. Far more troubling to realize that it was *this* woman who tempted him like no other.

Melena Walsh would continue to tempt him for as long as she remained in his care, under his dubious protection.

He didn't know how a woman who'd come into his life so unexpectedly—not to mention temporarily—was making him hungry for things that would come with a very permanent price.

"You're just going to walk away then?" She stood beside the bed, watching him prepare to make his escape. For a long moment, she said nothing more, her silence ripe with hurt and confusion, almost too much for him to bear. "You're not even going to acknowledge what almost happened just now?"

That he was only an instant away from taking her vein between his teeth? Or that every particle of his being was so ravenous for a taste of her Breedmate blood, there was a chance he might still act on the powerful impulse?

The memory of her blood scent hadn't left him since he'd first caught a trace of it back in the cave. He knew what she would taste like: caramel and dark, ripe cherries. On top of the other decadent sweetness that still lingered on his tongue from his carnal exploration of her body.

Lazaro cursed roundly, a nasty profanity spoken in a language only the eldest of the Breed like him would comprehend.

"No, Melena, I'm not going to acknowledge it." He caught her gaze, knowing how cold his own must look through her eyes. Yet even as he glowered, furious with his own lack of control, his traitorous body had lost none of its interest in her. "And yes, I am going to walk away, and what happened here will not happen again."

She stared at him. "I think we both know better than that. You still want me, Lazaro. I don't need to read your aura to see that."

"This was a mistake," he snarled through teeth and fangs. "I damned well won't complicate it any more by letting it become something both of us will regret forever."

He turned and walked out the door.

Before his shaky resolve could break completely.

CHAPTER 8

True to his word, he didn't return.

She had showered and dressed, even eaten a fresh meal that Jehan had brought up to her sometime after Lazaro had gone. That was hours ago, according to the old grandfather clock in the hallway. It was well into the evening before she'd finally given up waiting, wondering...God, pitifully hoping, that he would come back and at least talk to her after the incredible passion they'd shared.

Her psychic gift prevented her from sulking over doubts about Lazaro's intentions. It wasn't that he didn't want her tonight. He'd left because he wanted her too much.

But that didn't change the fact that he was quite obviously avoiding her.

She'd since begun pacing the residential suites in the clothing he bought for her, feeling like a prisoner in a beautiful, unlocked cage. Although she had the entire fourth floor to explore, decency kept her from snooping too avidly through

Lazaro's home. Not that she'd find anything very personal in his quarters, she'd realized fairly quickly.

Each room was consummately appointed with elegant furnishings and a variety of fine things. Sophisticated pieces, tasteful antiques, a wealth of heirloom Oriental rugs—the kind of things she might expect someone who'd lived as long as him would appreciate.

But there was nothing personal in Lazaro's home. Nothing modern.

There were no photographs on the bureaus or sofa tables or walls. No mementoes scattered about in any of the meticulously kept rooms. There was nothing to remind him of the past century, let alone the past twenty years.

He lived here in a carefully curated, elegant isolation.

Her conversation with Jehan and Savage came back to her now. The fact that Lazaro had never fully gotten over the deaths of his mate and family. That he blamed himself for not being able to save them. And so he'd joined the Order and exiled himself to this place.

If he hadn't found room in his heart for anything or anyone in the past two decades, how could she hope he might let her in after just a couple of days?

She had half a mind to confront him about the way he was living his life. Maybe it wasn't her place to call him on it. Maybe she'd be better off leaving well enough alone and simply wait to return home to the States, where she had her own life to manage.

A life that no longer included her father, she thought, swamped with a fresh wave of grief to think that Lazaro's entry into her life came at the loss of someone else she loved. But even before losing her father last night, even before the loss of her dear mother years before, Melena realized that her life was missing something vital.

She had a life that, if she were truly being honest with herself, wasn't so much different from the cage Lazaro had built around himself here in Rome.

She had a nice apartment of her own at her father's Darkhaven in Baltimore. She had friends. She had lovers when she wanted them. She had colleagues at her father's office and in the GNC. She had her Breed brother, Derek. She had a full life and plenty of companionship whenever she needed it.

And yet, deep down, she was so lonely.

She saw that same emptiness in Lazaro. Maybe he saw it in her too. Maybe that's why when their gazes had locked in the midst of their release tonight, the connection had felt so real. So nakedly, startlingly real.

How could he expect her to ignore that as if it hadn't happened?

She couldn't.

And she wouldn't, not without a fight.

Whatever was building so swiftly—powerfully—between them had a chance of growing into something extraordinary. She felt that with a certainty in her bones, in her blood. And she knew she wasn't alone in that feeling.

So, like it or not, Lazaro Archer was simply going to have to talk to her. He might be accustomed to blustering and bossing his way around everyone else in his life, but she wouldn't stand for it.

Steeling herself for a battle she wasn't sure she could win, Melena left the suite on the fourth floor and headed downstairs to the mansion's main level. It was quiet down there, so she continued on, toward the connected command center of the estate.

She didn't get far.

From out of nowhere, a massive wall of muscle materialized to block her path.

It wasn't Lazaro. Not Savage or Jehan either.

She looked up and found herself gaping into the cold, hard face of the one warrior she hadn't yet met. His shaved head and jagged scar made him look even more lethal than the dark stare he held her in now.

He didn't speak. Didn't seem inclined to make even the remotest effort to put her at ease.

Melena lifted her chin in defiance. "I'm looking for Lazaro."

"He's not here." God, that voice was coarse gravel. "And you shouldn't be down here either, female."

As he spoke, Savage and Jehan came out of a nearby chamber in the corridor. Sav hissed. "Trygg, for fuck's sake. Go easy on her. Save the venom for tonight's patrol."

When the scarred vampire didn't so much as twitch in acknowledgment, Jehan stepped forward, placing himself between Melena and the warrior who bristled with a feral darkness.

Jehan squared off against his comrade, gently guiding Melena behind him. "I'm only going to say it once. Back. The. Fuck. Down."

The one called Trygg had an aura that verged on feral. The menacing haze sent a shiver up Melena's spine. She saw pain there too, buried deep, but it was a dangerous pain, as sharp as razorblades.

For a long moment, Trygg didn't move. Neither did Jehan. It wasn't clear which warrior would be the first to spill the other's blood, but there was no mistaking that cool, calm, and cultured Jehan was every bit as lethal as his barely leashed brother-in-arms.

Perhaps more so. Jehan's aura burned with a steady,

unyielding resolve. He would be unstoppable in all things he set out to do. Honorable to his last breath.

Trygg seemed to know this about his teammate. He seemed to respect it. With a slow exhale, the terrifying Breed male let his shoulders relax a degree. His jaw pulsed, but he did as his comrades demanded, easing back on his heels with a quiet rumble in his throat.

Then he turned and walked away, stalking down the far length of the corridor.

"You okay?" Sav asked.

Melena nodded. "Is his problem just me, or does he despise all women?"

Sav gave her a sardonic look. "It's not just you. And it's a long, ugly story. If you have a week or five to spare, maybe I'd tell you."

No, she didn't have that kind of time. And the fact that tomorrow Lazaro would be taking her back to the States put a pang of regret in her breast. She wanted to stay a bit longer with Savage and Jehan.

She wanted to get to know them: Savage and his easy charm and gorgeous smile. Jehan, with his intriguing past and enigmatic personality. She wanted to know what obligation awaited him in Morocco, and why was he trying to outrun it. Against her own sense of logic or self-preservation, Melena also wanted to stay long enough to understand what had inspired Trygg's terrifying animosity toward women.

And Lazaro...

Would there ever be enough time in this life to unravel all of his torment and secrets and dark, hidden thoughts? Would he even allow her that, if by some miracle they did have more time? All those rooms of his upstairs, missing memories...she wanted to help him fill them back up again.

She wanted to be the one to save him this time.

"Come on," Sav said. "You really shouldn't be down here in the operations compound. Lazaro will have our balls if—"

The warrior's words cut short as a gust of cold, dark air seemed to blow in from the far end of the corridor. He was there. Melena waited to hear Lazaro growl his fury at the men, or demand to know what she was doing back in the Order's domain after he prohibited her from distracting his team.

But he didn't growl or demand anything. He just stared at her in silence, his sapphire gaze trained on her alone.

Intense. Penetrating. Focused on her with searingly sensual regard.

She trembled a little under that potent gaze, not from anything resembling fear. Seeing him there, looking at her as though no one and nothing else existed but the two of them, it was all she could do to keep from launching herself at him from down the corridor and flying into his arms.

But Melena held back. And now she noticed that there was something different about him tonight. Something different in the relaxed state of his *glyphs*, in his schooled expression.

"You were gone for a long time," she murmured. And then she did start to approach him, though not with the jubilation she felt just a moment ago. This was something heavier. Something that stung as the realization began to dawn on her. "You've fed. You went out to find a blood Host. A woman?"

He didn't deny it.

Damn him, he just stood there, watching impassively as she slowed to a stop in front of him. The array of skin markings on his arms under his rolled-back sleeves were calm, satiated. "Did you fuck her too, Lazaro?"

Behind her, Melena heard Jehan quietly clear his throat. There was brief movement in the corridor at her back, followed by the polite closing of a door as the two warriors made a hasty exit.

"Did you?" she repeated, now that it was just she and Lazaro in the passageway.

He swore, roundly, fiercely under his breath. "Don't be ridiculous."

She scoffed. "You know what's ridiculous? Sitting around waiting for you to return. Hoping that I didn't somehow push you away tonight. But how can I push you away when I never had you in the first place?"

She swept past him on a wounded, furious cry. She didn't know if he followed. In that moment, she didn't care.

But he had followed her. She had only made it to the main floor of the mansion's residential wing when Lazaro halted her by grasping her hand. "Melena—"

"You know what else is ridiculous?" she fumed at him. "Hoping you'd come back and tell me that you realize there's something serious going on between us too." She glanced away, giving a shake of her head. "It's ridiculous to expect that a man who's been living his life like a ghost for twenty years could ever admit that he actually feels something again."

Wrenching out of his light hold, she ran for the stairs. She heard him stalking up behind her, but he didn't stop her now. Her breath was heaving by the time she found herself in the center of Lazaro's palatial living room suite.

"I don't want another blood bond, Melena. I won't risk it." His deep voice sounded brittle at her back. "So, whatever you think is happening here between us, it has no future."

"Whatever I think?" She turned to face him. It stung that he wanted to diminish what they'd shared, but she didn't believe him. She could see that he cared. But he was also determined to push her away. He truly intended to spend the rest of his life alone, punishing himself for something he couldn't control. "I know about your family, Lazaro. I know you blame yourself for not being there to save Ellie and the rest of your Darkhaven."

He glared at her furiously, as if she had violated some boundary simply in speaking of the incident. "They trusted me to keep them safe. I failed them."

"You weren't there. That's all. And that's a completely different thing."

"No, not to me. And if you know so much about it, then you should also understand why I left to find a blood Host tonight. After making love with you, if I'd stayed..." He exhaled sharply. "The ifs don't matter. I don't want another Breedmate shackled to me and reliant on me for protection, for her sustenance. For her life. I won't do that to someone again. I prefer to keep my appetites restricted to human females."

Melena scoffed. "Safe women you can fuck and feed from without the risk of feeling anything."

He stared, unflinching at her jab. "It is simpler that way, yes."

"Women who leave you free to walk away and wallow in your guilt and self-flagellation."

His full lips had compressed in a flat line as she spoke, his expression hardening now. "That's right, Melena. That's exactly the kind of woman I prefer. Simple. Safe. Forgettable. What I don't want is what nearly happened between us today. I'm not going to sacrifice two decades of resolve on a couple of days of passion."

And she didn't want to hear him say that. No more than she wanted to acknowledge the regret she saw in his dark gaze, or the grim determination that emanated from the stormy color of his aura. "How fortunate for you and your martyred honor that I'll be out of your life tomorrow."

She pivoted away from him on a burst of hot anger and bitter pride.

She didn't even make it two steps.

Lazaro was suddenly in front of her. And he was fuming. He seized her shoulders, blocking her path with the muscled wall of his body and the power of his sudden fury.

Amber sparks crackled in the midnight-blue pools of his eyes as his gaze clashed and locked with hers. "The fact that you'll soon be out of my life is fortunate for you too, Melena." He drew in a breath and more fire leapt into his irises, reducing his pupils to thinning, inhuman slits. "You should be thanking me for my restraint thus far, not stomping off to pout like a petulant child."

"Let go of me." He didn't. If anything, his grip only went firmer. His face was so close to hers now, the bones of his high, angled cheeks sharpening with the emergence of his fangs. She refused to shrink under the full blast of his Gen One fury. "You call it restraint, the fact that you deny yourself the things you really want? Do you honestly think your guilt is ever going to release you if you only keep feeding it with your self-imposed isolation and pointless, hollow honor?"

A snarl curled up from his throat. It escaped through bared teeth and fangs. "You're far too young to lecture me on life and death or guilt and honor. You don't have any idea what you're talking about."

"Don't I?" she challenged hotly. And maybe a bit recklessly too, but she was so pissed off at him now, she couldn't stop. "Twenty years of licking your wounds, hiding from life? Pretending you don't need anything or anybody? One of us is acting like a sulking child, but it sure as hell isn't me."

A low, thunderous growl. That was all the warning she had. Then Lazaro's mouth came down hard on hers. His kiss was ruthless, punishing. Spiked with raw fury and violent need.

Melena felt his fangs press against her lips, against her tongue when she opened her mouth to his invading kiss. He was holding nothing back now. She felt that hard intent roll through him with the fierce drumming of his heart against her breasts. She felt it in the steely demand of his cock when he brought his arm around her back and hauled her into a brutal embrace, crushing her abdomen into the immense ridge of his arousal.

She felt the wall come up against her spine and realized dazedly that he had moved her there using the power of his Breed genetics to propel them both across the floor in an instant. Lazaro fucked her mouth with his tongue, grazed her lips with the deadly points of his fangs. His big body caged her, allowing her no room to escape, even if she tried.

"Now tell me what you know about my restraint, Melena." His voice had dropped to a timbre so low, so dangerously dark, everything reasonable and sane in her trembled with a dreadful anticipation. His merciless gaze bore into her, daring her to flinch as he bent his head toward her vulnerable throat. "Tell me about my hollow honor."

She couldn't speak. All of her senses were drawn taut, coiled to the point of breaking. His breath rushed hot and fevered across her neck, into the sensitive shell of her ear. Her pulse was racing, electricity coursing through her veins everywhere Lazaro touched her. He reached up, ran his fingertips over the scarlet teardrop-and-crescent-moon mark at the base of her throat.

"Tell me you're not afraid that I'll take your sweet, frantic carotid in my teeth right now and do exactly what I've been dying to do since I first saw you on that boat last night."

She was afraid. And for all her desire for him—despite her sense that she had been waiting all her life for him and had never realized it until now—Lazaro's fangs nestled so dangerously near her throat put an arrow of true panic in her blood.

If he pierced her vein, just one sip of her Breedmate blood would create an exclusive, unbreakable bond. He would be tied to her for the rest of his days—or until her death, should that come sooner.

One sip and he would crave no one else.

He would always feel Melena in his blood, even if they were apart. Even if miles or entire countries separated them.

One sip and there would be no other Breedmate for him, even if he drank from another woman with the mark after his connection was formed with Melena.

And if she drank from him in exchange, their bond would be a complete circle. Sustaining. Eternal. Unbreakable, except by death.

Melena held her breath, suddenly understanding the full impact of what she was inviting. Lazaro Archer, one of the eldest, most formidable Gen One Breed males in existence, his body pressed against her from breast to ankle, his enormous fangs bared and poised over her carotid.

And he wanted *her.*

Every muscled inch of him was coiled with power, all of it at the razor's edge of breaking. Desire burned in his eyes—desire for her body and for the vein that throbbed so madly near his mouth. Heat and rigid strength pulsed where his pelvis ground so demandingly into her abdomen.

He was feral and wild and nearly unhinged...and she had never known anything hotter in her life.

"Damn you for making me want you," he muttered thickly. His searing breath skated across her electrified skin like a lick of flame. "Damn you for making me want this..."

She heard his brief inhalation. Felt his head descend, his lips and tongue sealing over her skin. Then she felt Lazaro's bite.

Sharp.

Deep.

Irrevocable.

CHAPTER 9

The first hot rush of Melena's blood over his tongue slammed into him like a freight train. Warm, rich, potent. And laced with the sweetest trace of caramel and dark, ripe cherries—her Breedmate blood scent, a fragrance that had tempted him from the moment he'd first encountered it. Now that scent would call him as surely as a divining rod seeking a spring of cool, pure water.

He would feel her in his blood, everything she experienced most intensely would now echo in his veins. Her joy, her sorrow, her fears. Her hungers. Melena owned him now.

The bond he'd just activated inside him was unbreakable. She had been a distraction to his mind, will, and body before; now she would be his lifelong addiction.

And although better than a thousand years' of logic strove to persuade him that Melena's blood was a shackle he shouldn't want and damned well didn't need, the part of him that was purely male, elementally Breed, roared with the one word Lazaro never thought he would utter again: *Mine*.

He had known this feeling before. But what he had with Melena now was all the more intense for how desperately he'd tried to resist it. He groaned with possessive pleasure, knocked off his axis with a force that staggered him.

Amazed him.

Holy hell, it humbled him.

He drank more, starving for her. Twenty years of feeding from human blood Hosts went up in flames as he drew greedily from Melena's tender vein. Her blood surged into his body, nourishing his cells as it wrapped silken bonds around his soul.

She was his. Even if his mind and will were reluctant to accept that fact, his body knew it with a ferocity he could hardly contain now. And where his desire for her had been consuming nearly from the moment he first laid eyes on her two nights ago, now it was a raging inferno that demanded its own satisfaction.

He wanted her savagely.

Needed her with a fury that left him shaking.

He realized in that moment that it wasn't only the blood bond that lashed her to him. Melena would have owned him even if he hadn't given in to his thirst for her tonight.

As unwelcome as that thought was—as unnerving as he found it, to think that she had obliterated his long-standing, iron resolve—it was a truth Lazaro could not deny.

And right now, he could not get enough of her.

* * * *

Oh, God, she was lost to this man.

She'd never known what it would be like to have a Breed male drink from her. Like so much where he was concerned, Melena hadn't been prepared.

With her head dropped back and Lazaro suckling with long,

hard tugs at her carotid, she dissolved into a state of pure, boneless bliss. She held him as he drank from her, cushioning his big body as he thrust against her where they stood.

Her veins were on fire. The core of her had gone molten as well. Each demanding pull at her throat sent arrows of pleasure and need shooting through every cell of her being.

When Lazaro suddenly stopped suckling her and swept his tongue over the wounds he'd made, Melena groaned in protest. "I need you naked now," he muttered thickly against her throat. "I can't wait much longer."

Neither could she. "Yes," she gasped, her hands still clutching at him as he began to sink down before her into a crouch. He made quick work of her slacks and panties, baring her to him with the clothing pooled at her feet. On a low growl, he moved in and kissed each hipbone, then descended farther, burying his face between her thighs. "Oh, God..."

His tongue cleaved her folds, hot and wet and hungry. In long, knee-weakening strokes, he lapped and suckled, then kissed and nipped, wringing a moan from her as he drew her clit into his mouth and teased it toward a frenzy. She felt his teeth graze her sensitive flesh, felt the sharp tips of his fangs getting larger as he feasted on her with ruthless abandon.

She was quivering with hard need, on the verge of orgasm already, as he slowly kissed his way back up her body. With a deep, rolling growl, he stripped off her sweater and bra, then tossed them aside to gaze on her nakedness with burning amber eyes. Her blood stained his sensual lips a duskier hue, making his diamond-white fangs stand out in stark contrast.

He had never looked more dangerous or inhuman...nor more preternaturally beautiful.

"Lazaro," she sighed, her voice feathery, as unsteady as her legs. That sigh became a moan as he lavished her breasts and nipples with his hands and mouth, tongue and teeth.

He muttered her name in a fevered, animal-like rasp that sent her blood surging with even greater pleasure and arousal. He needed her now, as much as she needed him. On a curse he released her nipple and drew back to shuck his pants and shirt. He stood before her like an otherworldly god.

Magnificent. Terrifying. And hers.

Melena reached down between their bodies to grasp the jutting length of his cock. His shaft more than filled her hand, thick and warm and pulsing with strength. He purred deep in the back of his throat as she stroked him, then seized her mouth in a wild kiss. She could taste herself on his tongue, her blood and juices an erotic sweetness that only made her burn even more for him. She stroked him harder, craved him with a desperate ache that demanded to be filled.

"I can feel your need in your blood, Melena," he rasped against her lips. "It's alive in me now. So fucking intense. Everything you feel this strongly, I will feel too." He flexed his hips, his shaft surging even more powerfully within the tight circle of her fingers. "I need to be inside you. Put me there."

She obeyed, guiding him into the slick cleft of her body. He drove home on a savage groan, the fierce thrust making her cry out in pleasure. He gave her more, slamming in hard and urgently, his lack of restraint sending her own control spiraling away. She clawed at him as he fucked her against the wall, orgasm roaring up on her in a shocking wave of sensation.

She came fast and hard, convulsing in tremors that racked her from head to toe. As she shattered around him, Lazaro's tempo became a storm. He crashed into her with abandon, his immense body taut and shaking, so deliciously wild. He cursed against the side of her neck as his own release roared up on him. She felt him go rigid, driving deeper with every stroke, until a wordless shout tore out of him and he released.

Melena registered the hot blast of his orgasm, a heat she felt in her core and in every tingling particle of her being. She was drained and completed all at once, awash in a pleasure that rocked her to her soul.

But Lazaro wasn't finished with her yet, apparently.

Instead of pulling out, he guided her legs up around him, lifting her against him, their bodies still joined and vibrating with the aftershocks of release. He brought her into the bedroom, placed her beneath him on the big bed.

Then he began to drive her mad with desire and pleasure all over again.

* * * *

The temptation to stay with her in his bed had been all but irresistible, but after hours of making love to Melena, Lazaro finally let her sleep. No easy thing, for how much he still craved her. His desire for her soft curves and addicting heat was rivaled only by his newer thirst for her.

He didn't want to think about how strong those urges were, now that he'd indulged so recklessly—selfishly—in both.

He didn't want to think about how right it felt to lie next to her, inside of her, to hear her soft cries of pleasure or the quiet puffs of her breath as she slept so sweetly—trustingly—in his arms.

He didn't want to think about any of that when reality waited for them in D.C. in just a few short hours.

Lazaro slipped away from Melena's side to shower and get dressed, the predawn morning a prickle in his ancient Breed veins as he headed down to the command center to meet with his team. The warriors were just coming in from the night's patrol.

Trygg said nothing as he approached with the others from the far end of the corridor. The brutal warrior merely strode into the team's meeting room for the mission review. Jehan and Sav both slowed as their path met Lazaro's in the passageway. They greeted him with measured nods and sober, suspicious gazes.

"How did it go out there?" Lazaro asked them. "Any rumblings on the street about the explosion on Turati's yacht?"

Jehan answered first. "Nothing that we found. It was just a typical night in the Eternal City. A couple of club brawls to break up before they got too bloody and created a bigger problem. Handful of Breed youths feeding past curfew near the train station."

"No unusual activity at all?"

Sav glanced down, trying to suppress a grin. "Seemed like the only unusual activity going on last night was in here."

Lazaro glared, but he couldn't take offense at the truth.

"Is everything all right, Commander?" Jehan asked, ever the diplomatic professional, despite being one of the most dangerous warriors Lazaro had ever seen. "The situation with Melena seemed...difficult."

Now, it was only more difficult. Not to mention complicated. If she had cause to despise him last night after he'd seduced her then fled to find a blood Host, she had every reason in the world to loathe him for what he did a few hours ago.

And for what he had yet to do, after he saw her safely home to the States.

"Melena Walsh's welfare is no one's concern here but mine," he said, eager to shut down the topic of discussion, even though it weighed heavily on him. "The Order has difficulties of its own to worry about. For instance, does it bother anyone else that no one is stepping forward to claim responsibility for the assassinations of Turati and Byron Walsh the other night? The attack smacks of Opus Nostrum, yet the group hasn't formally declared it was their doing."

"Maybe they're waiting for the right time to own up to it," Savage suggested.

Jehan grunted, not quite convinced, if the shrewd look in his sky-blue eyes was any indication. "If it is Opus, maybe it wasn't a sanctioned attack. Maybe it was an over-zealous member looking to make a name for himself among his comrades. Or maybe it was done for more personal reasons than that. Turati was a high-profile businessman with political connections as well. He could've had any number of enemies. The same could be said of Walsh."

Lazaro gave a grim nod. The warrior could be right about any of those scenarios. And the only thing more troubling than Opus making such a bold move was the thought of a renegade agent operating from his own agenda.

Walking into the meeting room with Sav and Jehan, Lazaro couldn't help but relive the shock and horror of the rocket's destruction. And the fact that Melena might have been part of the carnage? That she had been mere seconds away from complete obliteration along with the others on that yacht?

Christ. What had shaken him that night—what had outraged him as a man and as the one entrusted with the security of those dead men—now put a cold knot of dread in his chest.

It put real, marrow-chilling fear in his bones.

Now more than ever, he needed to ensure she would be kept far out of harm's reach. And as bitter as the taste was on his tongue, he knew that anyone in the Order's orbit, or in that of the ever-expanding number of enemies seeking to incite true war between man and Breed, would always be at risk.

Like Ellie had been.

Like their sons and the dozen other family members living in Lazaro's Darkhaven who were killed on his watch.

He couldn't bear to have anything happen to Melena. She'd been through enough pain and loss already.

And so had he.

As Lazaro took his seat at the head of the conference table in the room with his men, Trygg palmed a slip of paper and slid it toward him. "What's this?"

Trygg nodded his shaved head at the note he'd scrawled. "Located her brother, like you asked." Lazaro glanced at the Baltimore, Maryland, address. "Derek Walsh is on a plane out of London as we speak. Booked the flight yesterday, after his father's death aboard Turati's yacht made international headlines."

Lazaro nodded gravely. He would've rather Melena's brother—Byron Walsh's only blood kin—had heard the news another way, but there was no fixing that now. At least her brother would be there for her. She would be home again, with family and familiar things. God knew, she had needed someplace soft to fall these past days, Lazaro thought grimly. And she hadn't exactly found that with him.

No, she'd found tears and anger and hurt.

She'd found a man ill-prepared to give her what she needed, what an extraordinary, tender-hearted woman like Melena deserved in life...and in love.

Instead of offering her comfort during her most vulnerable state, he'd growled and snapped at her. When he wasn't busy seducing her, that is.

When he wasn't selfishly slaking all of his needs on her as if he would ever be worthy of her heart or her blood.

He had no business giving in to those urges when war was

still brewing all around him. So long as there were enemies killing innocents, his duty was, and always would be, to the Order. How could he have let himself slip so egregiously when it came to Melena? How could he be letting himself fall in love when he knew all too well how easily it could be ripped from his arms at any moment?

Love...

Fuck. Of all the rash impulses he had been unable to resist when it came to Melena, that would be the most foolish of them all.

Loving her would be even more selfish than the blood bond he had no right to claim and no intention of completing.

CHAPTER 10

Lazaro was gone when she woke up that morning.

He had stayed away most of the day, vanished to his command center until the time came for Melena and him to leave for the flight to D.C. that afternoon. Even on board the Order's private jet, Lazaro had remained distant, his comm unit to his ear most of the time, or his attention rooted to his work and his computer. She would have called him preoccupied, but his smoky aura had conveyed a deliberate resistance.

Hours later and thousands of miles away from everything they'd shared in Rome, Melena had sat beside him in the debriefing with Lucan Thorne and a few other members of the Order at the Washington, D.C., headquarters, feeling almost as though she were seated next to a polite, detached stranger. He'd introduced her graciously, almost formally, giving no one cause to suspect she was anything more to him than a civilian temporarily placed in his safekeeping following the attack on Turati's yacht.

He was careful not to touch her, even though heat crackled

between them at the slightest brush of contact. He was careful not to let his gaze linger too long, even though his indigo eyes smoldered with awareness every time he glanced her way. He was coolly, determinedly remote.

It had made her want to scream.

She still felt that swamping urge, having since been removed from the meeting to accompany some of the Order's women in the living room of the headquarters' elegant mansion while the warriors continued their discussion in private.

"Are you sure you wouldn't like something to drink or eat, Melena?" Lucan Thorne's auburn-haired Breedmate, Gabrielle, offered a warm smile as she indicated a side table laid out with plates of finger sandwiches and tea cakes. Aromatic Darjeeling and chamomile steeped in their pots next to an elegant white china service.

Although her appetite wasn't there, everything looked and smelled delicious, and Melena was reluctant to reject the woman's kindness. "Thank you, I think I will have a little something."

She walked over from the sofa, joined by Gabrielle and two other women of the Order.

All of the Breedmates present tonight at the headquarters had been nothing but kind and welcoming. They were a family. That much was clear. And in the short time she'd been sitting with them, they'd each done their best to make Melena feel at home among friends as well.

Melena had been exhausted from her session with Lucan and the other warriors, to say nothing of the dread she felt every time she looked at Lazaro. Being around other women had helped dissolve some of that anxiety, even if it might only be for a little while.

She couldn't help watching the hallway outside, waiting for

some indication that the meeting had broken so she and Lazaro could finally go somewhere to speak privately. So she could get rid of the awful feeling she had that he was somehow already gone.

Gabrielle handed her a small plate, collecting Melena from her dark thoughts. "If you'd like something more substantial, Savannah made a big pot of jambalaya earlier today. You really can't go wrong with any of her amazing cooking."

"I do have my numerous and varied talents," Savannah said, her doe-brown eyes dancing at the compliment. The beautiful, mocha-skinned Breedmate was bonded to Gideon, another of the warriors present tonight. Where her big blond-haired mate had an intense, slightly mad genius quality about him, Savannah exuded tranquility and smooth confidence.

As Melena put a few cucumber sandwiches and peach tarts on her plate, she found it next to impossible to keep from staring at the third woman in the room with them—the one mated to the warrior named Brock. Jenna looked like neither of her Breedmate companions. In fact, Melena didn't think she was a Breedmate at all, though she definitely wasn't fully human either.

Tall and athletic, Jenna wore her brown hair cropped close to her scalp. She was pretty, yet formidable in some indefinable way, and when she leaned across the sideboard to pour a cup of tea, Melena noticed an intricate pattern of skin markings at her nape. Skin markings that looked remarkably, impossibly, similar to...

"Are those tribal tattoos, or—"

"Not tattoos." Jenna's hazel eyes were smiling, but there was a note of seriousness in her voice. She turned to provide a better look. The array fanned out to cover the back of Jenna's neck, disappearing beneath the collar of her shirt. The arcs and swirls tracked upward too, well into her hairline and up the back of her skull. From the looks of it, they continued down Jenna's spine and onto her shoulders as well.

"They're *dermaglyphs*." Melena frowned, astonished and confused. Females born Breed had been unheard of for millennia. They might never have come into existence if not for the genetic experimentations conducted in Dragos's labs in the decades before he was killed by the Order. Even then, there were only a handful of women known to bear the *glyphs* and blood appetites of the Breed.

Melena found herself staring harder now, watching Jenna pile her plate with a healthy assortment of sweets and sandwiches. "You can eat all of that?"

Jenna grinned. "I'll probably come back for seconds."

"I'm sorry," Melena blurted, immediately feeling stupid and rude for letting her curiosity overrule her manners. "I just thought..."

"You thought I was Breed?" Jenna popped a tiny pastry in her mouth and gave a shake of her head. "Not quite. But I haven't been fully human for a long time either. I guess as long as Brock loves me, it doesn't matter where I end up. Together we can handle anything—and we have."

Her two friends nodded in agreement, and Melena smiled even though the sentiment was bittersweet for her. She'd believed she and Lazaro were heading toward something special like that too. Her father's death was still a raw ache in her heart, and would be for a very long time. The attack she'd narrowly survived still held her in a cold grasp. But Lazaro had helped her through.

He'd been her rock, her comfort, whether he wanted to accept that role or not. And ever since they'd left Rome, she felt that support slipping away. No, she felt pretty damned certain that he wasn't slipping—he was running away. Cutting her off with his forbidding silence and maddening stoicism.

When she finally heard his deep voice approaching with Lucan and the others, Melena's heart started pounding in a heavy, expectant tempo. She didn't know whether to be relieved or terrified when he strode to the threshold of the drawing room and those penetrating dark blue eyes found her, locking on with the intensity that would probably always kindle an instant heat in her blood.

"Melena. May I have a word with you." Not a question, not an invitation. A sober demand.

She rose and walked to meet him as the rest of the group fell into easy conversation behind them. Lazaro led her down the hall to another formal parlor. He carefully closed the door, keeping his back to her for longer than she would have liked.

Melena didn't have to see his impassive face to know he was about to crush her heart when he finally turned around to look at her. His aura was a dark cloud, the shuttered gunmetal gray from before.

Before the first time he'd touched her, kissed her.

Before he'd shown her such incredible passion and tenderness when he made love to her. And when he bit her vein and took her blood into his body, into his soul.

All of those moments seemed to evaporate as she looked at him now. They became nothing under the regretful look in his ageless eyes.

But the moments they had weren't nothing. He'd felt everything she had. He wanted her. He cared for her. He cared maybe even as much as she did for him. She could see that diamond-bright truth breaking through the muddy resistance of his aura.

Everything they'd shared in Rome had meant something

powerful and extraordinary to him too. But it wasn't enough.

"Why?" she murmured, her throat dry as ash.

He didn't pretend not to understand. "I told you from the beginning, Melena. I wasn't looking for this. I don't have a place for this in my life."

"For *this*," she said. "You mean, for me. For us."

He gave a somber nod. "For everything you deserve. For everything I can't give you."

"I don't recall asking you for anything, Lazaro. I didn't even ask for your heart."

"No, but you have it," he admitted quietly. "I think you owned a piece of my heart from the night I first dragged you out of that frozen pond in Boston."

"Then why?" Damn him, but those gentle words hurt all the more when she knew she was about to lose him. "Why are you pulling away from me now? Why are you acting as if I don't mean anything to you?"

He held her gaze, his own haunted and filled with remorse. "Because it isn't fair to you, letting you think I could ever be any kind of mate worthy of you."

She couldn't help herself. She scoffed brittly. "A shame you didn't arrive at that realization before you drank my blood."

"I told you I wasn't looking for a bond, Melena." His tone was tender but firm. As resolute as his aura. "I knew I couldn't give you that promise."

"No. Because you prefer simple arrangements. No entanglements or complications. No one to tempt you into throwing away twenty years of resolve on a couple of days of passion. Isn't that what you said?"

He said nothing for a long moment, staring at her grimly. "I'd resisted the temptation for a very long time, Melena. And it was easy. Until I found you."

Maybe she should have been moved by the confession. Maybe, if he hadn't been standing there giving her all of his reasons for why he was intent on breaking her heart. Instead, she thought back on everything they'd said to each other in heated anger and passion last night.

It was true, he had tried to resist her. He'd tried to push her away before he lost his damnable restraint. She hadn't helped, but she wasn't the one pretending she could walk away from what they had—from what they might be able to build together as a couple.

Lazaro had tried to warn her that he wasn't a hero come to save the day.

He tried to warn her that she might not be safe in his arms.

And she'd ignored him every time.

Yet for all his rigid honor and long-lived control, he hadn't been able to stop himself from claiming her.

He'd pierced her vein, swallowed her blood...created a bond that no other woman would ever be able to break for as long as Melena drew breath.

And wasn't that a convenient benefit of his colossal slip of self-discipline?

"Did you use me, Lazaro?"

His ebony brows crashed together. "Use you? Christ, no. Melena, you can't possibly think that—"

"Two decades of denial gone after just two days," she reminded him. "And now, with my blood living inside you, you'll never be tempted by another Breedmate. You have no ability to bond with anyone else as long as I live, so when you walk away from me now, you're free. Free as you've never been all this time. Congratulations. I'm so pleased I could permanently scratch that annoying itch for you."

He moved so fast she couldn't track him. One moment he

was several feet away at the closed door of the room, the next he was crowding her with his big body, his hands clamped around her biceps. His eyes flashed with furious amber.

"You are not an itch I needed to scratch." His voice rumbled, low and deep and hard with outrage. "Damn it, Melena. Don't say that. Don't ever believe that."

"Then what are we doing? You've been shutting me out since we left Rome. If you care for me—and I know you do, I can see it, I can feel it—then why are you pulling away?"

"Because I can't do this again. You know loss, Melena, but you don't know what it is to lose a mate. I don't ever want to know that pain again. And with you—" He blew out a harsh curse. "I've seen you nearly die twice. I don't want to know what that would feel like now that your blood lives inside me. And I don't want to be the reason you're not safe. My life is committed to the Order now. It's a dangerous life. I won't put you in the crossfire."

"Don't you think that's something I should decide for myself?"

He stared at her for a long time, silent but unswaying. "I'll see you home safely to Baltimore tonight. Your brother should already be there as well."

"You've talked to Derek? When?" Despite the fact that her heart was breaking, it perked at the mention of her brother. "Where is he? How is he? Does he know I'm okay?"

Lazaro shook his head soberly. "There was no time to contact him before we arrived. Trygg found him on a flight coming in from London tonight."

"I need to see him," she murmured. "Derek needs to know that I'm alive."

"Yes," Lazaro agreed. "We can leave as soon as you're ready."

"Then what?" she asked cautiously. "What about you?"

"Then I'll be returning to Rome."

"When?" she asked, although her dread already knew that answer.

"I leave tonight. Arrangements have already been made. The Order's jet is refueling and waiting for me to return a few hours from now."

"So soon." She exhaled sharply. "I imagine you must be eager to unload your burden and get on with your life."

"Don't think this is easy for me," he said, frowning as he brought his hand up to stroke her cheek. "It would be easier to stay, or to bring you back with me to the command center in Rome. It would be the easiest thing in the world to fall in love with you, Melena."

She swallowed hard, trapped in his bleak, tormented eyes. Afraid to believe he might love her already. Afraid he never would.

He let his hand fall away. "It's become far too easy to imagine you at my side, as my mate. But those are things I can't give you. I can't ask you to risk your life by coming into my world. People die around me. I can't allow myself to be responsible for anyone else's life—your life. Don't you understand?"

"Yes, I think I finally do." The realization settled on her with clarity now, and not a little rage. "You're not doing this out of concern for me at all. You're doing it because you're afraid. I thought you were being noble by denying yourself another blood bond all this time. I thought it was honor that made you refuse to let another woman into your heart—and I think I loved you even more because of that. But I was wrong, wasn't I? You're pushing me away now because you're scared. You're running away from something that could probably be pretty fucking amazing because you're terrified of feeling any kind of pain again. The only person you're concerned about taking care of is yourself."

He didn't deny it. He didn't try to defend or justify anything she said. He let out a slow exhalation. His jaw was set and rigid, his aura uncompromising. "Whenever you're ready, I'll take you home to your family's Darkhaven."

"No, don't bother. You're not responsible for me, remember? I'll find my own way home." She tried to walk past him and he grabbed her arm, misery smoldering beneath the resolve in his dark blue eyes. "Let me go. That's what you want, so I'm giving it to you."

"Melena..."

She wrenched out of his loose grasp. "Good-bye, Lazaro."

This time, he didn't stop her. He stood unmoving, unspeaking, as she stepped around him and walked out the door.

CHAPTER 11

An hour later, Melena sat woodenly in the passenger seat of the Order's SUV as it rolled up to her family's Darkhaven in Baltimore. The big brownstone should have been a welcome sight in so many ways, yet all she felt was sorrow when she looked at it through the tinted glass of the vehicle's window.

Sorrow that she'd never hear her father's voice inside the house again. Sorrow for the pain her brother must be feeling as he walked into the empty home, believing he'd lost not only his father but Melena as well. She didn't want to imagine Derek's anguish, being the sole blood kin of Byron and Frances Walsh, both gone now.

And yes, Melena felt sorrow for herself too. Because instead of facing all of these heartaches with Lazaro's strong arms around her and his love to hold her up if she crumbled, she would be doing it alone.

"I'm ready," she murmured, more to herself than the Breed male behind the wheel.

Lucan and Gabrielle's son, Darion, put the vehicle in park

and turned a sympathetic look on her. "I'll walk you inside, Miss Walsh."

"No." She shook her head, warmed by the kind offer. Darion was as gentlemanly as he was attractive. "Thank you, but that's not necessary. My brother won't be expecting me, and I don't imagine it will be easy for him when I walk in the door and he sees that I'm alive. I'd rather do this on my own."

"Okay." Darion frowned, but gave her a nod. The dark-haired Breed male's aura was golden and kind, steadfast with the strength of a born leader. "But I'm gonna wait here until you've gone inside."

She reached over to touch his large hand. "Thank you."

Melena climbed out of the vehicle and headed up the walkway toward the front door. It was unlocked, the soft light in the vestibule a warm, welcoming beacon. She stepped inside and pivoted to wave good-bye to Darion. As the black SUV rolled away, she took a steeling breath and closed the door behind her.

She was home.

She was back on safe, familiar ground. And yet, as she walked quietly through the house, she felt like a stranger to the place. Like a ghost drifting through a life that no longer quite fit anymore.

She drifted past the front rooms and grand central staircase, unsure if she should call to Derek or wait and let him adjust to seeing her once she found him.

She didn't have long to wonder. She heard her brother talking farther down the hallway. In her father's study. Derek was on a call with someone, the low rumble of his voice drawing Melena with a relief and a comfort she definitely needed right now.

"Yes, sir, the shipment is en route and everything is in order. That's right, I saw to it personally."

Melena paused at the open doorway. Derek stood with his back to her, dressed in loose sweatpants, his brown hair still wet from a recent shower. He wasn't wearing a shirt, and although the sight of her Breed brother's *glyphs* were no surprise to her, something did make her breath catch abruptly in her throat.

Derek now sported a number of tattoos on his broad back and shoulders. Unusual-looking stars, crossed swords, some kind of black beetle—a scarab, she realized, confused by the body art that hadn't been there the last time she saw her brother. He must have gotten the tattoos after he'd moved overseas a year ago.

"It should be in your hands tomorrow, Mr. Rior—" Derek's voice dried up.

He realized he wasn't alone now. Disconnecting the call without a word of excuse, he smoothly slipped the phone into his pants pocket.

When he pivoted around, his face was slack with shock...with stark disbelief.

"Melena. My God." He frowned, gave a vague shake of his head. But he didn't rush over to embrace her. He didn't react the way she would have expected at all from a sibling who loved her, worried for her. "I don't understand. The news reports said there were no survivors. I thought you were..."

"Dead," she replied, only understanding in that instant why her brother seemed less than relieved to see her.

He hadn't expected to see her again at all.

His sickening aura told the truth. It hovered around him, oily with corruption. Foul with deceit.

"It was you, Derek." She could hardly form the words, could hardly reconcile what her senses were telling her. "You were the faceless, hidden betrayer he feared. Oh, my God...it was you who arranged for our father's death."

* * * *

Lazaro boarded the Order's private jet in a hellish mood.

He hadn't expected the conversation to go well with Melena, but damn if he anticipated the kind of pain that had lodged itself in his chest from the moment she stormed away from him. That ache was still there, cold and gnawing, creating a vacuum behind his sternum that he didn't imagine would ever be filled.

She was gone.

He'd made certain of that—for her, he wanted to reassure himself. But Melena's words still echoed in his mind. Her condemning, all-too-accurate accusation.

He was a coward.

As the jet began to taxi toward the runway, Lazaro couldn't dismiss the feeling that he was walking away from the best thing that had happened to him in a very long time.

And why?

Because of exactly what Melena said. He was afraid. Afraid to his marrow that he might let himself fall in love with her and risk cutting his heart open again should anything happen to her.

The truth was, he was already falling. Letting her go cut him open, and as he rubbed at the empty ache in his chest, he realized only then what a fucking idiot he was.

Pushing Melena away had been the most cowardly act of his long life.

He'd lived more than a thousand years. He had loved a woman deeply, fearlessly, for several centuries before he lost her. He knew what real love felt like. He knew himself well enough to understand that time, for him, was immaterial. Time could last forever, or it could be gone in the blink of an eye.

He loved Melena. And whether it had happened in a matter of days, or over the span of a hundred years, it was all the same to him. He wanted her beside him. Starting right now, if she would have it in her heart to forgive him.

On a snarl, he punched the call button next to his seat.

"Yes, sir?"

"Turn it around."

The pilot went silent for a moment. "Sir, we're next on the runway to taxi and—"

"Turn this goddamned plane around. Now." On second thought, he couldn't wait that long. He unbuckled his seat belt and stood up. "Never mind. I'm getting off right here."

"But, sir—"

He unlocked the hatch and leapt down from the fuselage onto the dark tarmac. Then he was running. Heading for the Order fleet vehicle he'd parked in the private hangar when he'd arrived.

It was just as he neared the black sedan that his senses suddenly seized up, gripped by something powerful and horrifying. His veins lit up with a piercing dread.

Not his emotions.

Melena's.

He could feel her terror rising in his blood through his bond to her.

Holy hell.

She was in danger.

She was in fear for her very life.

CHAPTER 12

Melena tried to run.

She wasn't even halfway into the hall before Derek yanked her off her feet. His hand wound tight in her hair. Pain raked her scalp as he hauled her face backward to meet his furious sneer.

"You're supposed to be dead, sister dear," he hissed against her cheek. "You and Father both in one fell swoop. I've been planning it since he confided in me about his meeting with Turati."

"You killed him, you bastard!" Melena could hardly contain her contempt or her fear. "You killed more than a dozen innocent people that night, Derek. My God, did you hate us that much or are you simply out of your mind?"

"Arranging for that rocket strike was the sanest thing I've ever done. Killing Father and Turati? Doing it while they were secreted away for a covert meeting to broker their precious fucking peace? Let's just say it won me all the respect I deserve with the people who really matter."

Melena's heart sank even further. "Opus Nostrum."

He chuckled. "I was a mere lieutenant for this past year. They barely knew my name. Now I've got a direct line to the inner circle. I'll be a part of that circle soon. This was my proof of allegiance, my demonstration of worth." Derek's eyes flashed with vicious intent as she fought against his ruthless, unyielding hold. "As for you, Melena, I couldn't very well let you see me after I joined the organization. Your irritating gift would've sniffed me out right away."

"You plotted to kill me all this time?" she asked, hating that his duplicity hurt her so deeply.

Derek shrugged, his crackling amber eyes roaming over her terrified, miserable face with a cold disregard. "At first, I thought I could just avoid you. But then Father confided in me that he'd been having premonitions of a betrayal, and I knew it was only a matter of time before one or both of you discovered my alliance with Opus Nostrum. When he later told me about the meeting and the fact that you'd be accompanying him, I knew it was my chance to act."

Bile rose in her throat as he spoke. "You're a cold-blooded murderer, Derek. You're a sick, backstabbing fuck!"

"Careful, little sister. I'm the only thing standing between you and your grave." He snagged a cord from the table lamp on the desk, sending the thing crashing to the floor. Then he quickly bound her wrists behind her back. "Don't rush me to put you in it."

With that, he wrenched her into a more punishing hold and shoved her forward. He guided her out of their father's study and down the opposite end of the hallway. Melena had no choice but to shuffle ahead of him, panicking when she realized he was taking her outside.

He walked her toward their father's GNC-issued silver SUV

parked in the drive.

"What are you doing, Derek?"

He opened the back door. Shoved her into the farthest seat.

"Where are you taking me?" she demanded, hysteria bubbling up as he calmly climbed behind the wheel. "If you're going to kill me, then just do it, damn you!"

"I'm not going to kill you, Melena." His cold eyes met her gaze in the rearview mirror. "I'm going to take you to my comrades in the organization. They're not nice people, I'm afraid. You're going to wish you died in that fucking explosion."

He started the engine. Then he backed away from the Darkhaven and started speeding for the highway.

* * * *

Lazaro gunned the black sedan through the late-night traffic on the highway, speeding like a bat out of hell for Baltimore. He didn't know what had Melena so terrified, but her fear was visceral. And it was eating him alive from the inside.

"Hang on, baby," he muttered as he dodged one lagging car and nearly sideswiped another. "Ah, God, Melena...know that I'm coming for you."

He was just about to veer toward the exit he needed when all of his instincts lit up like fireworks.

She was somewhere close—right now.

Possibly on the same stretch of highway, by the way his veins were clanging with alarm bells.

He scanned both sides of the divided lanes, a chaos of headlights and commuting vehicles. She might as well be a needle in a goddamned haystack.

And then—holy shit.

His Breed senses pulled his attention toward a light-colored

SUV that had just merged on to the opposite side of the highway. The vehicle was speeding almost as fast as he'd been. In a big fucking hurry to get somewhere.

Melena.

She was inside the silver SUV. He knew it with total, marrow-chilling certainty.

And whoever had her was going to have bleeding hell to pay if she'd been harmed in any way.

Lazaro yanked the steering wheel and sent the sedan roaring into the median. Grass and mud flew in all directions as he tore across the divider and launched his car into the traffic on the other side. He floored the pedal, tearing up the pavement as he tried to catch the bumper of the vehicle that held his woman.

Flashing his lights, laying on the horn, he tried to get the attention of the vehicle bearing GNC diplomatic plates. It belonged to Byron Walsh, but Lazaro wasn't certain who the Breed male was behind the wheel. But then, as he ran up alongside it briefly, he caught a glimpse of the driver. A cold, sickening recognition set in.

Son of a bitch.

Derek Walsh.

And judging from the vampire's murderous glower, he had no intention of giving up Melena without a fight. The SUV lurched into a more reckless speed. It careened behind a semitrailer, dodging between a car of teens and a commuter bus. Lazaro could only follow, negotiating the traffic and keeping his focus trained on his quarry.

Walsh drove erratically for several miles with Lazaro chewing up his bumper. More than once, there was the opportunity to ram the bastard and send the SUV rolling, or to draw one of his semiautomatics and blast a hole in the Breed male's skull...but not with Melena inside. Not when Lazaro's heart was tied to her and every breath in his body was devoted to keeping her safe.

He hissed when Walsh narrowly avoided a collision with a car drifting into his lane. And when another near-miss snapped off the SUV's passenger side mirror, Lazaro shouted a furious curse. He saw a break up ahead—a chance to get in front of Walsh and force him into the median. Lazaro buried the gas pedal and flew past.

But Walsh saw the maneuver coming.

Instead of letting himself catch up to Lazaro, he hung a hard right and gunned it for an upcoming exit.

An exit that was under construction, littered with barrels and an obstacle course of concrete barriers.

Walsh was going too fast, too frantically.

Lazaro stomped on his brake and was whipping around to give chase again when the SUV clipped one of the barriers and went airborne, rolling into a hard crash.

All the breath seemed to suck out of Lazaro's lungs in that instant. The entire world seemed to stop breathing. Dust went up in the darkness, the haze illuminated by the beams of passing vehicles on the road.

Then, a spark of flame.

"No," Lazaro moaned, his blood screaming for Melena. "Goddamn it, no!"

He threw his vehicle in park on the shoulder and hit the ground running.

Even with his preternatural speed, he'd barely gotten within arm's reach of the wreck before the ruptured gas tank ignited. A blinding wall of flames shot skyward, heat blasting his face.

"Melena, no!"

* * * *

She couldn't breathe.

Heat all around her. Splitting pain in her skull, ringing in her ears. She opened her eyes and saw a churning, thickening cloud of gray smoke. And flames.

Oh, God. Fire everywhere.

Melena tried to move, but her arms wouldn't work. Her wrists were tied. She remembered now, awareness coming back to her. Derek had bound her. He'd driven away with her.

He and his Opus Nostrum comrades were going to kill her.

"No," she gasped, choking on smoke and heat. "Oh, my God...no!"

She started kicking, screaming, trying frantically to get free of the restraints. She couldn't loosen them. And something was crushing her in the back of the SUV. She looked up and saw the floor. Beneath her, the roof of her father's GNC vehicle.

The smoke was rolling in front of her eyes, burning them. She couldn't keep her lids open. Hurt to see, to breathe...

"Melena." The deep voice penetrated the fire and sooty air that surrounded her. She wanted to reach for it—for him—but she was trapped, unable to move. "Melena, I'm going to get you out of here, sweetheart. You stay with me, damn it!"

There was a great, groaning howl as the vehicle rocked where it had fallen. A gust of cool air, followed by a rush of hot, intensifying flame.

"I'm coming in to get you," Lazaro said.

She couldn't see him, but she felt him climbing inside the inferno. Crawling all the way to the back, where she lay broken and half-conscious.

And then she felt his strong hands make contact with her.

"Ah, Christ," he hissed, and she knew what he saw couldn't be good.

Another metallic roar filled the air, then the crushing weight that had pinned her down was lifted. Tenderly, Lazaro took hold of her. Started pulling her free of the wreckage.

"I've got you now, Melena. I've got you."

She didn't let the first sob go until she felt the warmth of his chest against her cheek. She buried her face in that comforting strength, breathed in the scent of him even as her throat screamed with pain from the smoke that choked her lungs.

And then he scooped her up in his arms and he was running. Away from the smoke. Away from the heat and the fire and the horror.

Cool night air enveloped her, filled her nose as she braved a cleansing breath. And circled around her were Lazaro's strong arms, holding her close, keeping her safe—carrying her away from certain death.

He set her down in the crisp, moist grass, while behind them came a jarring roll of thunder as a plume of fire and smoke shot up into the moonlit sky. Horns blared out on the highway. Tires screeched as traffic came to a halt at the scene of the accident.

But all Melena knew was the haggard, terrified face of the man she loved, staring down at her as he held her in a careful embrace. He tore off the lamp cord that bound her wrists and tossed it aside on a vicious snarl. When he reached down to smooth a hank of limp hair from her face, his fingers trembled.

Melena tried to speak but couldn't push sound through her lips. Her body ached everywhere, some of the pains searing, others a dull, relentless throb.

Lazaro's dark eyes were sober in his handsome face. His beautiful, sensual mouth was a flattened, grim line. "You're going to be all right, you hear me? I'm not letting you go."

She wanted to argue that he already had. That her heart was still breaking from the thought of him pushing her out of his life. Out of his heart.

He stared down at her, misery swimming in his gaze. "I'm not going to lose you, Melena."

On a curse, he brought his wrist up to his mouth and bit into his own flesh. No hesitation. No asking for permission before he put the punctures to her parted lips. "Drink."

She tried to shake her head. This wasn't the way she wanted him, coming back to save her when he had been determined to leave her. Whether he did this out of some noble sense of obligation or guilt, or simply under the power of his bond to her, she didn't want it. Not like this.

She wanted to reject the gift of his blood, of his bond, but the instant the wet, spicy warmth came in contact with her parched tongue, she greedily drank him in.

And oh, it was incredible.

Lazaro's Gen One blood flowed down her throat like pure light. She felt it strengthening her body, feeding her cells. Mending her injuries.

He tipped his head back on a strangled moan as she swallowed more of his eternal gift, his fangs gleaming, his broad shoulders and immense body silhouetted by the flames he'd walked through to save her.

It was the last thing Melena saw before a bone-deep exhaustion rose up to claim her.

CHAPTER 13

He had lived for more than a thousand years, long enough that few things still held the power to amaze him. The sight of Melena finally opening her eyes to look at him, after lying in bed unconscious for two days, was one of those rare pleasures for Lazaro Archer.

The worst of her injuries had healed. Her burns were gone. She was alive, and he'd never seen anything more welcome in all his life.

He smiled at her and gently stroked his thumb over the back of her hand as he held it. "Hello, beautiful."

"Where are we?" she asked, her voice thready.

"Still in D.C. I brought you here after the accident. I've been waiting for you to wake up so I could ask you something."

"My brother," she murmured.

Lazaro shook his head. "I'm sorry, Melena."

"He was part of Opus Nostrum," she said quietly. "He arranged for the attack on Turati and my father to prove something to his superiors. He was trying to win their recognition. And he was afraid if I ever saw him again, I'd know all of his secrets."

Lazaro and the Order had already surmised that Derek Walsh likely had ties to Opus, but hearing Melena confirm it made his blood seethe with renewed rage. "If he'd survived the accident the other night, I swear, I would've killed the bastard myself."

"He seemed so different. He'd only been away for a year, but he wasn't my brother anymore. And he had strange tattoos I've never seen before. Symbols of some kind, and a black scarab on his back."

"A scarab?" Lazaro thought back to conversations he'd had with Lucan and the other warriors. Reports out of London about human bodies in the morgue bearing the same kind of unusual tattoo.

"Does it mean something?" she asked, worry creasing her brow.

"It might," Lazaro said, seeing no reason to shield her from his world. But he would bring her into that part of his life slowly, after they returned to Rome. If she would be willing, that is. "We need to talk about what's happening with us, Melena. About our bond."

She turned her head on the pillow, looking away from him. "You shouldn't have done it. You didn't need to come back to save me."

"Yes, Melena, I did." He reached out, catching her chin on the tips of his fingers. He brought her gaze back to him. "Do you think I could've left, knowing that you were in danger? I feel you in my blood now."

"I'm not your obligation, Lazaro. I won't be your burden or a regret you'll carry around forever."

"No, you won't," he agreed solemnly. "But will you be my

mate?"

She stared at him for a long moment. Then slowly, she shook her head. "No. No, I can't do that. You're only saying it because your honor compels you to."

He swore a harsh curse. "Melena, listen to me. See me. I know you can read my intent, so open your eyes and hear me out. I love you. I want you in my life, by my side. Forever, if you'll have me."

"What about everything you said before? You didn't want another mate under your protection. You didn't want that responsibility ever again."

He blew out a bitter laugh. "And as you so accurately pointed out for me, I was being a coward and an idiot."

"I don't think I said you were an idiot," she murmured, looking up at him from under her long lashes.

"Well, I was. And as soon as I realized that, I came after you."

"Because you were worried about me. You knew I was in danger and your blood wouldn't let you stay away without trying to help me."

"No, Melena. Because I love you." He stroked her cheek. "And because I realized the only thing worse than loving you and dreading that I might know the pain of losing you in the future, was the idea of losing you now. Before we've even begun to know what we can have together."

He leaned over her on the bed and kissed her tenderly, deeply, with all the love in his ageless heart. "I love you, Melena."

"And I love you," she whispered. She held his gaze, her own so open-hearted and trusting, it took all of his control to keep from crushing her in a fierce embrace. "You've saved my life three times now. If I'm going to be your mate, that means you're going to have to let me save you sometimes too."

"Oh, love," he murmured. "Don't you know? You already have."

Sign up for the 1001 Dark Nights Newsletter
and be entered to win a Tiffany Key necklace.

There's a contest every month!

Go to www.1001DarkNights.com to subscribe.

As a bonus, all subscribers will receive a free
1001 Dark Nights story on 1/1/15.
The First Night
by Shayla Black, Lexi Blake & M.J. Rose

Turn the page for a full list of the
1001 Dark Nights fabulous novellas...

1001 Dark Nights

FOREVER WICKED
A Wicked Lovers Novella
by Shayla Black

CRIMSON TWILIGHT
A Krewe of Hunters Novella
by Heather Graham

CAPTURED IN SURRENDER
A MacKenzie Family Novella
by Liliana Hart

SILENT BITE: A SCANGUARDS WEDDING
A Scanguards Vampire Novella
by Tina Folsom

DUNGEON GAMES
A Masters and Mercenaries Novella
by Lexi Blake

AZAGOTH
A Demonica Novella
by Larissa Ione

NEED YOU NOW
A Shattered Promises Series Prelude
by Lisa Renee Jones

SHOW ME, BABY
A Masters of the Shadowlands Novella
by Cherise Sinclair

ROPED IN
A Blacktop Cowboys ® Novella
by Lorelei James

TEMPTED BY MIDNIGHT
A Midnight Breed Novella
by Lara Adrian

THE FLAME
A Desire Exchange Novella
by Christopher Rice

CARESS OF DARKNESS
A Phoenix Brotherhood Novella
by Julie Kenner

WICKED WOLF
A Redwood Pack Novella
by Carrie Ann Ryan

HARD AS STEEL
A Hard Ink/Raven Riders Crossover
by Laura Kaye

STROKE OF MIDNIGHT
A Midnight Breed Novella
by Lara Adrian

Also from Evil Eye Concepts:
TAME ME
A Stark International Novella
by J. Kenner

Acknowledgments from the Author

Several years ago, my editor at Random House forwarded me an email from a reader who'd just discovered my books and then tore through the entire Midnight Breed series in a matter of a week. Those are my favorite kinds of emails, and what made this one even more special was it came from the wife of a bestselling thriller writer whose books I also happened to love!

What a thrill and an honor it is to now call the lovely Liz Berry a dear friend, and a wonderful colleague. I'm delighted to be part of the 1001 Dark Nights collection with this novella in my Midnight Breed vampire romance series. My thanks to Liz, MJ Rose, Jillian Stein, my fellow authors and friends in this collection, and everyone else working behind the scenes to make the project possible. Can't wait to do it again next year!

Heartfelt thanks, as always, to my family, friends, and colleagues, and to my readers. None of my books would be possible without all of you!

With love,

Lara Adrian

About Lara Adrian

LARA ADRIAN is the *New York Times* and #1 internationally best-selling author of the Midnight Breed vampire romance series, with nearly 4 million books in print and digital worldwide and translations licensed to more than 20 countries. Her books regularly appear in the top spots of all the major bestseller lists including the *New York Times, USA Today, Publishers Weekly*, Indiebound, Amazon.com, Barnes & Noble, etc.

Lara Adrian's debut title, Kiss of Midnight, was named Borders Books bestselling debut romance of 2007. Later that year, her third title, Midnight Awakening, was named one of Amazon.com's Top Ten Romances of the Year. Reviewers have called Lara's books "addictively readable" (Chicago Tribune), "extraordinary" (Fresh Fiction), and "one of the best vampire series on the market" (Romantic Times).

With an ancestry stretching back to the Mayflower and the court of King Henry VIII, Lara Adrian lives with her husband in New England, surrounded by centuries-old graveyards, hip urban comforts, and the endless inspiration of the broody Atlantic Ocean.

Connect with Lara online:

Website: http://www.laraadrian.com/
Facebook: https://www.facebook.com/LaraAdrianBooks
Twitter: https://twitter.com/lara_adrian
Pinterest: http://www.pinterest.com/laraadrian/

Was this your first taste of Lara Adrian's Midnight Breed series? Start at the beginning with the prequel novella, available now in ebook and trade paperback

Here's a preview!

A TOUCH OF MIDNIGHT
By Lara Adrian

Chapter 1

Boston University
October, 1974

Savannah Dupree turned the silver urn in her gloved hands, studying its intricate engravings through the bruise-colored tarnish that dulled the 200-year-old work of art. The floral motif tooled into the polished silver was indicative of the Rococo style of the early and mid-1700s, yet the design was conservative, much less ornate than most of the examples shown in the reference materials lying open on the study lab table in front of her.

Removing one of the soft white cotton curator's gloves meant to protect the urn from skin oils during handling, Savannah reached for one of the books. She flipped through several pages of photographed art objects, drinking vessels, serving dishes and snuff boxes from Italy, England and France, comparing their more elaborate styles to that of the urn she was trying to catalogue. She and the three other freshman Art History students seated in the university's archive room with her had been hand-picked by Professor Keaton to earn extra credit in his class by helping to log and analyze a recent estate donation of Colonial furnishings and artifacts.

She wasn't blind to the fact that the single professor had selected only female students for his after-hours extra credit project. Savannah's roommate, Rachel, had been ecstatic to have been chosen. Then again, the girl had been campaigning for Keaton's attention since the first week of class. And she'd definitely gotten noticed. Savannah glanced toward the professor's office next door, where the dark-haired man now stood at the window, talking on the phone, yet staring with blatant interest at pretty, red-haired Rachel in her tight, low-cut sweater and micro-miniskirt.

"Isn't he a fox?" she whispered to Savannah, a row of thin metal bangle bracelets clinking musically as Rachel reached up to hook her loose hair behind her ear. "He could be Burt Reynolds' brother, don't you think?"

Savannah frowned, skeptical. She glanced over at the lean man with the shoulder-length hair and overgrown moustache, and the mushroom-brown corduroy suit and open-necked satin shirt. A zodiac sign pendant glinted from within a thick nest of exposed chest hair. Fashionable or not, the look didn't do a thing for Savannah. "Sorry, Rach. I'm not seeing it. Unless Burt Reynolds has a brother in the porno business. Plus, he's too old for you. He must be close to forty, for crying out loud."

"Shut up! I think he's cute." Rachel giggled, crossing her arms under her breasts and tossing her head in a move that had Professor Keaton leaning closer to the glass, practically on the verge of drooling. "I'm gonna go see if he wants to check my work. Maybe he'll ask me to stay after school and clean his erasers or something."

"Mm-hmm. Or something," Savannah drawled through her smile, shaking her head as Rachel waggled her brows then sauntered toward the professor's office. Having come to Boston University on a full academic scholarship and the highest SAT scores across twenty-two parishes in south central Louisiana, Savannah didn't really need help bolstering her grades. She'd accepted the extra credit assignment only out of her insatiable love for history and learning.

She looked at the urn again, then retrieved another catalogue of London silver from the Colonial period and compared the piece to the ones documented on the pages. Doubting her initial analysis now, she picked up her pencil and erased what she'd first written in her notebook. The urn wasn't English in origin. *American*, she corrected. Likely crafted in New York or Philadelphia, if she were forced to guess. Or did the simplicity of the Rococo design lean more toward the work of a Boston artisan?

Savannah huffed out a sigh, frustrated by how tedious and inexact the work was proving to be. There was a better way, after all.

She knew of a far more efficient, accurate way to resolve the origins--all the hidden secrets--of these old treasures. But she couldn't very well start fondling everything with her bare hands. Not with Professor Keaton in his office a few feet away. Not with her other two classmates gathered at the table with her, working on their own items from the collection. She wouldn't dare use the peculiar skill she'd been born with.

No, she left that part of her back home in Acadiana. She wasn't about to let anyone up here in Boston think of her as some voodoo freak show. She was different enough among the predominantly white student body. She didn't want anyone knowing how truly strange she was. Aside from her only living kin--her older sister, Amelie--no one knew about Savannah's extrasensory gift, and that's how she intended to keep it.

Much as she loved Amelie, Savannah had been happy to leave the bayou behind and try to make her own path in life. A normal life. One that wasn't rooted in the swamps with a Cajun mother who'd been more than a shade eccentric, for all Savannah could recall of her, and a father who'd been a drifter, absent for all of his daughter's life, little better than a rumor, according to Amelie.

If not for Amelie, who'd practically raised her, Savannah would have belonged to no one. She still felt somehow out of place in the world, lost and searching, apart from everyone else around her. For as long as she could remember, she'd felt...*different*.

Which was probably why she was striving so hard to make her life normal.

She'd hoped moving away to attend college right out of high school would give her some sense of purpose. A feeling of belonging and direction. She'd taken the maximum load of classes and filled her evenings and weekends with a part-time job at the Boston Public Library.

Oh, shit.

A job she was going to be late for, she realized, glancing up at the clock on the wall. She was due for her 4PM shift at the library in twenty minutes--barely enough time to wrap up now and hurry her butt across town.

Savannah closed her notebook and hastily straightened up her work area at the table. Picking up the urn in her gloved hands, she carried the piece back into the archive storage room where the rest of the donated collection's catalogued furniture and art objects had been placed.

As she set the silver vessel on the shelf and put away her gloves, something caught her eye in a dim corner of the room. A long, slender case of some sort stood propped against the wall, partially concealed behind a rolled-up antique rug.

Had she and the other students missed an item?

She strode over to get a better look. Behind the bound rug was an old wooden case. About five feet in length, the container was unremarkable except for the fact that it seemed deliberately separated--hidden--from the rest of the things in the room.

What was it?

Savannah moved aside the heavy, rolled rug, struggling with its unwieldy bulk. As she leaned the rug against the perpendicular wall, she bumped the wooden case. It tipped forward suddenly, about to crash to the floor.

Panicked, Savannah lunged, shooting her arms out and using her entire body to break the case's fall. As she caught it, taking the piece down with her onto her knees, the old leather hinges holding it together snapped apart with a soft *pop-pop-pop*.

A length of cold, smooth steel tumbled out of the case and into Savannah's open hands.

Her bare hands.

The metal was a jolting chill against her palms. Heavy. Sharp-edged. Lethal.

Startled, Savannah sucked in a breath, but couldn't move fast enough to avoid the prolonged contact or the power of her gift, which stirred to life inside her.

The sword's history opened up to her, like a window into the past. A random moment, fused forever into the metal and now exploding in vivid, if scattered, detail in Savannah's mind.

She saw a man holding the weapon before him as in combat.

Tall and menacing, a mane of thick blond waves danced wildly around his head as he stared down an unseen opponent under a black-velvet, moonlit sky. His stance was unforgiving, the air about him as grim as death itself. Piercing blue eyes cut through the tendrils of sweat-dampened hair that drooped into the ruthless angles of his face and square-cut jaw.

The man was immense, thick roped muscles bulging from broad shoulders and biceps beneath the loose drape of his ecru linen shirt. Smooth, fawn-colored trousers clung to his powerful thighs as he advanced on his quarry, blade poised to kill. Whoever the man was who'd once wielded this deadly weapon, he was not some post-Elizabethan dandy, but a warrior.

Bold.

Arrogant.

Magnetic. Dangerously so.

The swordsman closed in on his target, no mercy whatsoever in the hard line of his mouth, nor in the blazing blue eyes that narrowed with unswerving intent, seeming almost to glow with some inner fury that Savannah couldn't comprehend. A dark curiosity prickled inside her, against her better instincts.

Who was this man?

Where was he from? How had he lived?

How many centuries ago must he have died?

Through the lens of her mind's eye, Savannah watched the warrior come to a halt. He stared down at the one he now met in mortal combat. His broad mouth was flat, merciless. He raised his sword arm, prepared to strike.

And then he did, driving home the blade in a swift, certain death blow.

Savannah's heart raced, pounding frantically in her breast. She could hardly breathe for the combination of fear and fascination swirling inside her.

She tried to see the swordsman's face in better detail, but his wild tangle of golden hair and the shadows of the night that surrounded him hid all but the most basic hints of his features.

And now, as so often happened with her gift, the vision was

beginning to fracture apart. The image started to splinter, breaking into scattered shards.

She'd never been able to control her ability, not even when she tried. It was a powerful gift, but an elusive one too. Now was no different. Savannah struggled to hold on, but the glimpse the sword gave her was slipping...fading...drifting out of reach.

As Savannah's mind cleared, she uncurled her fingers from their grip on the blade. She stared down at the length of polished steel resting across her open palms.

She closed her eyes and tried to conjure the face of the swordsman from memory, but only the faintest impression of him remained within her grasp. Soon, even that was slipping away. Then it was gone.

He was gone.

Banished back to the past, where he belonged.

And yet, a single, nagging question pulsed through her mind, through her veins. It demanded an answer, one she had little hope of resolving.

Who was he?

Also from Lara Adrian

Midnight Breed Series

A Touch of Midnight (prequel novella)
Kiss of Midnight
Kiss of Crimson
Midnight Awakening
Midnight Rising
Veil of Midnight
Ashes of Midnight
Shades of Midnight
Taken by Midnight
Deeper Than Midnight
A Taste of Midnight (ebook novella)
Darker After Midnight
The Midnight Breed Series Companion
Edge of Dawn
Marked by Midnight (novella)
Crave the Night
Tempted by Midnight (novella)
Bound to Darkness (Summer 2015)
...and more to come!

Masters of Seduction Series

Merciless (novella in Volume 1)
TBA (novella in Volume 2, April 2015)

Phoenix Code Series
Cut and Run (Nov 2014)
Hide and Seek (Spring 2015)

LARA ADRIAN writing as **TINA ST. JOHN**
Dragon Chalice Series
Warrior Trilogy
Lord of Vengeance

On behalf of 1001 Dark Nights,
Liz Berry and M.J. Rose would like to thank ~

Doug Scofield
Steve Berry
Richard Blake
Dan Slater
Asha Hossain
Chris Graham
Kim Guidroz
BookTrib After Dark
Jillian Stein
and Simon Lipskar

8/17 (10 4/17

Made in the USA
Middletown, DE
22 November 2014